GYPSY HEARTS

Other books by Lisa Mondello:

Her Heart for the Asking
His Heart for the Trusting
The More I See

GYPSY HEARTS

•

Lisa Mondello

AVALON BOOKS
NEW YORK

PRINTED IN THE UNITED STATES OF AMERICA
ON ACID-FREE PAPER
BY HADDON CRAFTSMEN, BLOOMSBURG, PENNSYLVANIA

To my parents, for loving and supporting me
no matter what road I chose.

Chapter One

Josie Tibbs sat behind the thick glass wall separating the control room from the studio. She listened to the same voice-over for the umpteenth time in the last hour and watched her client, Victor Clyde, owner of Clyde's Dog Emporium, as his face screwed into a frown.

Darn it, she thought, stifling the groan that was making its way up her throat. She'd rather eat a dog bone than record one more take of this dog food commercial.

"I don't know," Clyde said yet again. "I don't think it is quite there. We're spending a lot of money on this ad campaign and it needs to be perfect."

Well, heck, it was perfect an hour ago. In fact, Josie would have deemed the whole radio ad perfection after the first take. It was dog food, for cripes sake!

"What seems to be the problem with this last take?"

"I sound a little flat." Victor Clyde was a stout man with gray hair thinning at the temples, and a nose that reminded Josie of a dachshund. He stood in the studio with headphones clamped over his ears, listening as the tape played again, and waved his arms theatrically. "I want it to sound exciting."

Exciting dog food. Well, there was something new. It wasn't like the guy was singing the Star Spangled Banner at the World Series. But hey, to each his own.

"To be perfectly truthful, Mr. Clyde, the sound is coming through crisp and clear in here. Maybe the problem is that you're hearing it through headphones, which is not the way your customers will hear it. Why don't you come into the control room and I'll set it up to go through the small speakers. It will mimic more of what the general public will hear when they're driving down the interstate and hearing it through the car radio."

His face seemed to brighten up with that idea. Josie said a prayer of thanks for small favors.

While she waited for her client to come around into the sound booth, she cued the last master tape to the take they'd just finished. She could have chosen any one of the thirty takes Mr. Clyde had already done and she was sure he wouldn't know the difference. Once she'd set up the sound to play through the small, makeshift car speakers sitting on the panel, she hit play and settled back in the chair.

Watching the look on good ol' Vic's face, she decided she'd been played and played hard by her manager, Brian. He knew exactly what he was doing by giving her this job.

"I've decided to throw you a bone and give you some real exposure, Josie girl," he'd said in that same condescending tone he always used with her. "You've been with us long enough and your work has been good. You can handle this one."

She'd argued it was time for her to move on to some bigger projects, work with musicians again and do some producing, but Brian had always held those coveted sessions close to his chest or given them to one of the other sound engineers. He left the bones for Josie.

The more time that passed, the more she wondered if it was time to get out of this business altogether. She wasn't as cutthroat as were some of the other engineers who did sound. Aside from the politics in the studio, she loved her work.

Glancing at Mr. Clyde and recalling the afternoon she'd just spent, Josie decided to qualify that she loved her work with a big, fat, *sometimes* behind it.

The tape ended and she quickly re-cued it to play again. As Mr. Clyde listened to the playback once more on the mini-speakers, she gathered plugs that she'd used during the session and wrapped them neatly around her arm to keep them from tangling. She liked a tidy sound room. There was nothing worse than hunting for what she needed when she was in the middle of a project.

To her relief, Mr. Clyde appeared satisfied with the final take.

"Thanks, little lady. I'll be sure to pass on a good word for you with your boss."

She smiled, glad the day was finally done. "Brian will be in touch."

Mr. Clyde propped his cowboy hat on his head and tipped it once. "It's been a pleasure."

As the door closed behind him, Josie sighed with

relief. It would only take her twenty minutes to straighten up the sound room, collect all the cables, mark the master reel and store it. What should have been an easy one-hour job had quadrupled into four hours. Dexter wasn't going to be too happy with her when she got home.

Josie heard the outer door squeak as it opened and then again as it closed. She groaned. *Please don't let him have a change of heart.*

"Did you leave something behind, Mr. Clyde?" she said, turning around and peeking into the control room.

But it wasn't the owner of Clyde's Dog Food Emporium. Instead, the man in the control room stood tall and lean, just staring at her. Slowly, he pulled off his hat and held it in front of him as he was probably taught to do as a child.

He was a cowboy, through and through, Josie thought. Not just a wannabe like so many she'd seen pass through over the years. And she could tell the difference. This man didn't need dirt under his fingernails or sun-baked skin to tell his story. Although, he had the latter and she was willing to bet if she got up close and personal with this cowboy she'd see the freshly scrubbed dirt and callused hands.

"I'm not Clyde," he said, his voice low.

"I can see that. Can I help you?"

He smiled one of those high voltage smiles she'd seen on men in the business before. It usually meant they were charming the pants off someone for something. She liked to think she'd become immune.

"If your name is Josie Tibbs you can. Is it?"

"Well, that depends."

He gave her a crooked smile. "On?"

"Are you selling something?"

He laughed and even though there was distance between them, she could see the mark that made him truly magnificent. He had a deep dimple creasing just one cheek. His right. And with that lopsided smile, it made his whole face transform into something incredible.

She was in trouble.

"I guess I am at that," he said.

And her stomach fell. Why couldn't he be wearing a blue suit? Why did she have to meet him here instead of as she walked the aisles of the grocery store or something equally boring and coincidental?

"I'm not interested," she said flatly and went back to what she'd been doing.

"You don't even know what I have to offer."

She eyed him again. "Sure I do. It may be wrapped up in a different package, but I've seen it before."

"Ah."

Cocking her head, she said, "What's that for?"

"Nothing. I've just heard that about you is all."

Something prickled the back of her neck. He wasn't some dog food storeowner looking for someone to produce an annoying radio commercial. He was a musician. That much she already knew. Josie could smell out a musician a mile away. And she'd sworn off musicians years ago.

"Blue suit," she muttered to herself.

"What's that?"

"Nothing. I suggest you go back to talking to whomever you've been hearing things from. Like I said, I'm not interested in what you're selling."

Brian had to have sent this guy. Another bone, she fumed inwardly. This man wasn't slick, but there was a touch of arrogance about him, wrapped coolly around his charm. He didn't need to have a woman tell him he was handsome with his blue eyes and crooked smile. He had appeal. No doubt about it. And a woman would give herself away easily after just five minutes with him.

Josie turned away and continued her task, reaching for the last cord. "If you're looking for Brian, he'll be back around eight-thirty tomorrow morning."

"I already talked to Brian. That's how I found you."

She snapped her gaze around to him. She searched his clear blue eyes for the teasing, the crooked smile that would give him away, but it wasn't there. He was serious. He'd come looking for her.

She tried not to show her surprise that even after he'd spoken to Brian, he was now standing here talking to her. Brian usually snatched up all the sessions with musicians.

It was just as well, Josie thought. Yeah, she wanted creativity in her work and she longed to produce again, but the work she had was steady and it paid the bills. And although dog food wasn't exciting, it sure didn't break hearts. She wasn't wrong about this guy, was she?

"I need a sound engineer."

No kidding. There had to be a reason Brian passed this guy off on her. Maybe he stunk, both musically and literally. Brian wouldn't spend more than two minutes with the man if that were the case.

"For what?"

"I need to do a demo for a record company."

So he *was* a musician. And he definitely stunk. Brian didn't waste his time dealing with amateur work and didn't want his name attached to it. She'd been complaining so much lately that he had decided to send the poor guy her way. Take his money, let the kid think he had a chance at the big time and throw Josie another bone all in one shot.

Another banner day at DB Sound.

Josie sighed as she walked over to the control room and joined him inside.

"What's your name?"

"Brock. Brock Gentry."

"Never heard of you. I know most of the bands around. Are you local?" Just because she'd sworn off musicians, it didn't mean she'd tossed her love of music to the wind.

"I've been mostly playing around Steerage Rock."

"Steerage Rock? There's nothing out that way but ranches."

"Don't I know it. But there are a few local spots. Nothing big."

She nodded, folding her arms across her chest.

"I haven't done too many gigs in the city," he continued. "That's what I'm gearing up to do once this demo is complete."

"Is it just you or do you have a band?"

"Just me. But I do have some regular players that I've been working with on and off for a while."

He was bigger than he'd seemed when she was standing in the studio looking at him through the glass, Josie thought. He held his cowboy hat in front of him with both hands as comfortably as she imagined he'd hold a guitar. Big hands, she noticed, with long, graceful fingers.

Darn but he was young too. They all were these days. Young and filled with bright ideas and dreams of making it big. He was just one more. He'd soon learn very few ever made it past a quick handshake standing outside the record company doors.

An amused smile lit his face when he caught her staring at him.

"Well," she said, clearing her throat. "Did Brian set you up on the schedule?"

Brock shook his head. "He said I needed to talk to you first. He said if I insisted on working with you, you'd have to fit me in since your schedule is already tight. Said he normally does studio sessions with musicians and your forte is working on commercials and audio books."

I'll just bet. "Did he?" She gave Brock a quick smile.

"But I told him I wanted you or no go. I want you to do sound on this. That's the only reason I came to this studio."

She wished her shock didn't show on her face, but Josie knew it did. And because it did, Brock laughed. There were a hundred studios between Steerage Rock and DB Sound Studio and Brock could have chosen any one of them. Some at half the cost of what he'd be dishing out to record here.

"What's the deal? Why me?"

"I heard the demo you did for Grant Davies a few years back."

It was Josie's turn to laugh. "That was about a million years ago. How did you come to hear that demo? I thought all the extra copies Grant didn't burn were taking up space in a landfill somewhere."

Brock tossed his hat to the table by the soundboard.

"You must have been fresh out of high school when you worked with Grant Davies on that project."

"Something like that. And you were fresh out of what? Diapers?"

He ignored her slight jab at his age. In reality, he was probably only a few years younger than her. "I've been listening to music a long time. I like your style. It's too bad Davies moved in the direction he went. I'm not a fan of his work these days."

Josie wanted to say she'd stopped being a fan of Grant Davies the day he'd broken her heart. But in truth, it had taken a while to get to that point. Musically, she couldn't agree more with the kid.

"Grant had a lot of potential. He's used it to his advantage."

Brock sputtered. "Well, he's made a name for himself. I'll give you that. But I favor his earlier work. The stuff you worked on."

She quirked a smile of pride and actually used one of the "f" words she hated. "I'm flattered. There aren't a whole lot of people who've heard his earlier work. Or care to."

"That's too bad. It's good. So what do you say?"

Josie sized him up. Time-wise, she couldn't have been more ready. In the five years she'd been working at the DB Sound Studio, she'd had plenty of days like today, thinking she couldn't handle doing one more commercial. It was easy work that didn't require a whole lot of creativity on her part. The hardest part was suffering through take after take while the Clyde's of this world made up their mind that the commercials she recorded on tape would make them millions.

The hours were good and the jobs were steady, but the creativity on her part was zero. She'd missed that. Like so many of the young faces that strode through those studio doors, hoping to make a demo that would shoot them straight to stardom, Josie had her dreams too. But she'd learned all too quickly that dreams had a way of fading when reality came knocking at your door.

"I'm late for an appointment."

It wasn't a total lie, but it did send a prickle of regret picking at Josie. Dex would take major exception to be considered an appointment. But then, her eight-year-old double-pawed tabby took exception to her treating him like the cat he was.

"Good-bye, Brock," she said, and turned to go back to what she was doing.

Brock took in Josie Tibbs and had to keep from acting like a fool. The woman was beautiful with her long brown curls and ocean blue eyes. He hadn't expected that. He'd been all set to come in here and convince her to work with him on this demo.

"Wait. Maybe we can talk about this later, say over dinner?"

She did a double take, her sleepy eyes getting wide so he could see their color fully. They were the color of the sea with gold flecks that reminded him of sunshine glimmering on the water. She was a few years older than him. He knew that from what little he'd been able to uncover about her background. And there was definitely something captivating about her that caught him off guard.

Brock swallowed. Major fool. He knew better than to

look at any woman and see only what was on the surface. His whole life he'd hated it when people assumed things of him. He wasn't assuming she was beautiful; Josie most definitely was. He just didn't want to have that overshadow his reason for seeking her out in the first place.

Josie Tibbs was a good sound engineer. He wasn't shining sunshine on her when he'd made the compliment. With so many musicians clamoring for their chance to be noticed by studio executives, Brock had heard a lot of knockoff bands trying to imitate the same sound as whatever was the current trend in music, hoping for the same success.

That wasn't the way Brock wanted to go. Based on what he'd heard of her studio work, he knew Josie was the ticket to getting the sound he envisioned for himself.

"Don't you think you're a bit out of your league, cowboy?" she said, her chin lifting just a fraction of an inch.

He laughed, tipping his hat. Darn if he didn't feel the blush creep up his cheeks. "No."

Cocking her head to one side, she smiled. "You forgot the ma'am."

He looked directly into her eyes and said, "No, I didn't. I wouldn't make that mistake."

"I have to go. I'm not sure why you're here and what you want from me, but Grant Davies was a long time ago. Brian should be able to help you out with what you're looking to do." She picked up his cowboy hat from the table and handed it to him.

"I don't think you've heard me right," he said as she started to walk away.

Turning back, she chuckled. "Look. I've seen a lot of

guys come into the studio over the last few years. I'm flattered." Good grief, she'd used it twice in one day. "Not many people remember the studio work I did with Grant. Unfortunately, the record company didn't agree with my vision and Grant seemed to share their opinion. If you really want to make something of yourself in the music business, you don't need me. You need someone who can give the record companies what they want."

"Now see, that's the reason I'm here. I don't want what they're looking for. What I want is you."

Chapter Two

Josie tried not to flinch at Brock Gentry's words. She'd heard them before. At one time, she'd even been naive enough to believe them. Oh, when had she become so jaded?

Sighing, she took a step toward him. "What makes you so sure of that?"

"Lady, you haven't been listening to me. I know what kind of music is coming out of Nashville these days. But I'm not looking to be some face on a bubble gum card. I just want to play my music my way. Like I said, I like your work. I think we can make something good together."

Josie's insides hummed with his words. It was all she could do to remember the vow she'd made to herself four years ago. She wasn't getting involved with another music man. She was steering clear. No way, no how. The only thing it brought to her was heartache good enough for inspiring song lyrics. She didn't want songs or words. She wanted a true man to love her. Some boring blue suit man who'd wear a tie and go to work every day and come home to her and her alone every night.

"Blue suit," she whispered to herself.

"I beg your pardon?" Brock's eyes twinkled with light at her slip.

"Nothing. You've got me intrigued. I don't see a whole lot of your type come into the studio. And even then Brian snatches them up before I get a chance to say a word."

"I gathered that about him. So what do you say?"

"I say I should have my head examined." Wasn't Brian always talking about some shrink he visited? She'd have to remember to get the name. If she was seriously contemplating working with this cowboy— and she was—she was going to need some serious help.

Sighing, she said, "See Brian about booking some studio time in the evening. That's all I have available. And just so you know, I charge double time for evening work, so I need you to understand that right off the bat."

"Understood."

"Tell Brian how many songs you'll be doing and whatever time he says you need to get the job done, tell him to book half. He has a way of broadsiding a person. He's good at it."

"I've got a lot of songs. Enough for at least a full CD, maybe more. I figure I might as well get them all down on tracks and give the record company its pick."

Nodding, she said, "I hope whoever is bankrolling this project knows what he's gotten himself into. I don't want to run out of funds halfway through the session." He was naive, this man with the sparkling blue eyes and a smile that could force a woman to make an utter fool of herself. She was going to have to watch out.

"It's covered. It won't be a problem."

"Great. I'll see you then."

"What about dinner?"

"Dinner's not part of this gig. I told you, I have plans." Dexter would love this. She was sure he'd love Brock Gentry too. There was something about the man, something that had her head turning to just look at him. It wasn't just that he was handsome with his sun-streaked hair, or how his lopsided smile tilted ever so slightly to give him that boyish charm. He was different than the other cowboys she'd seen come strutting in through these studio doors. Sure, he had the twinkle in his eye, the dream of something big. But what was life without that dream?

Oh Lord, she was in trouble. *Blue suit, blue suit.*

She fought hard not to have the sudden breathlessness she felt show. But she feared Brock Gentry saw it anyway. "Why don't you leave me a few tapes in the office, kid," she said, packing up her things. It would do her good not to even look at him. "I'll listen to them, see where you're going, and then we can talk again when we get into the studio."

She lifted her head and saw the smile of triumph on his face.

"Thank you," he said as he tipped his hat. "And just so we're clear—I'm not a kid."

She stuffed her sweater into her bag, not bothering to fold it neatly, and looked at him. "I know," she said.

And she headed for the door before she made an even bigger fool of herself.

Brock sat on the black leather sofa in the control room, twiddling his thumbs as Josie worked around the studio, plugging in lines to the control room panel. He hadn't been able to get his mind off the woman in the last few days. He'd been so focused on finding Josie Tibbs and then getting her to agree to work with him that he hadn't thought at all about his reaction to her.

And boy what a reaction. He'd met pretty women before, sure. There was a certain attraction that had women gravitating to him regardless of the man he was. It was the image, the idea of being with a country singer. It didn't matter that he wasn't famous or even if he was any good. None of them seemed to look beyond that to see the man. He was just a face and a name. Someone they could swoon over when he stepped off the stage. They didn't really care about his music or what he wanted from it, what it meant to him. They just wanted the image. That always left him cold.

He'd watched Josie earlier as she listened to some of the rough demo tapes they'd made from some live performances back in Steerage Rock, the town he'd lived in his whole life, embarrassed by the crude sound and technical difficulties. But when it was over, Josie just smiled and said, "Let's get to work."

What that meant, he wasn't quite sure. At any rate, he was eager to get some tracks down and get to singing some of the songs he'd written over the last few years while he'd perfected his craft.

She was keeping her distance. That much Brock was

sure of. Every time he walked into the control room, Josie seemed to move in a different direction. He reasoned he should just stay the heck out of her way. He'd sought her out for a purpose and he had to let her do what she did best. But the woman was like a magnet pulling him to her.

"I hope you didn't get too bored," she said, coming into the sound room.

"Not at all."

She nodded. "We have a break room where clients usually hang out while I do some of the more tedious setup. We even have some arcade games in there to help pass the time."

He shook his head. "If it's all the same to you, I'll stick around and see how things are done in here."

She gave him a quick smile and shrugged. "Okay. Well, if you're going to be hanging around in here, I'm going to put you to work."

"Your wish is my command."

Josie tried to concentrate on her work. But with every move she made, she felt Brock's piercing blue eyes following her. It shouldn't have affected her at all, she thought as she dropped the master reel onto the tape player. She'd had attention from men before. In this business, there was always someone with a quick come on and enough sweet charm to put a sensible girl in a love-struck coma.

But there was something about the way Brock was watching her. There was interest in his eyes as they followed her, an eagerness, anticipation even, as if they were both part of doing something great.

And he was interested in her. She wasn't quite sure if that interest only went as far as his admiration for her work with Grant Davies or if it were fueled by something more personal. Josie wasn't sure which one she wanted more.

The early part of the session moved by quicker than Josie had anticipated which went a long way toward keeping her attention focused on what she was doing. Laying the music tracks could sometimes be tedious. Unlike her work doing commercials, she always wanted to get the music right. That meant spending the time up front to get a clean, crisp sound and then letting the musicians do their thing. Her job was to make their sound come alive without producing the life out of it.

Brock was alone in the studio, sitting on a stool in front of the microphone she'd set up. All the musicians had gone through a few songs earlier, laying the basic tracks. Now it was time to add Brock's vocals. Given the hour of the evening, the rest of the band members had all decided to head home for some sleep rather than sticking around to hear how the vocals blended in with the music. That left Josie alone with Brock, leaving nothing to separate them but the thick glass wall between the control room and the studio.

"I wrote this one the other day. I hope you like it," Brock said, the headphones covering his ear.

It was important to him that she like his music. Why that would make a difference, she wasn't sure. She'd seen Brian work with musicians before. They all wanted their egos stroked and no one was better at that than Brian. But it wasn't heartfelt. Brian couldn't care less as long as the session was paid for in full.

But it meant something to Brock. As he looked at her from the other room, she could see it in his eyes.

Josie cued the tape and pushed the record button. The sound of his guitar came over the speakers. Their eyes locked. With his hand holding one side of the headphones, Brock began to sing.

She loved his deep, smooth voice. The sound of his words as he sang plucked at her heartstrings as if he were strumming the steel strings of his guitar. Poetic and sincere. She couldn't help but wonder about the woman the song was so obviously written about. It was a song of new friendship, new love that seemed to have always been.

So deep into the song, Josie hadn't been paying attention to the meters at all. She had no clue if any of the levels had peaked. And when the song had ended and the music died down, she was startled when Brock pulled off the headphones and just smiled at her.

"You liked it, didn't you?" He didn't need to question that she had indeed loved the song. She knew it was written all over her face. It was then she realized she was still staring at him like an idiot.

Shaking off the feeling, she dragged her gaze away to the control panel. Her hands were trembling as she hit the buttons to rewind the tape and then punched the play button.

"Why don't we listen to how it sounds in here?" she said. This time she'd pay more attention to what she was doing instead of to the man who was driving her insane.

Blue suit. Blue suit.

Brock pulled a chair from the desk and sat next to

her, listening to the song replay. Once again, she was drawn into it.

"It's beautiful. You must have loved her very much," Josie whispered. Or still do, she thought with a pang of envy.

He turned to her, his deep blue eyes filled with emotion and she knew he did. But he didn't confirm her suspicion. He swallowed and said, "I can do this a little better."

"Do you think that's a good idea?"

"You don't?"

She shrugged slightly. No one was watching them. She almost wished the studio players were still in the game room playing with a pinball machine instead of home in their beds. It was just the two of them now, and the silence of the studio was wrapping around them in a way that made her wonder if it was such a good idea to agree to work with Brock Gentry.

"Sometimes too many takes pulls the life and emotion out of a song. Sometimes that first take is the best simply because it's raw, powerful with true feeling."

"I think it's missing something. Something didn't come through."

She simply nodded. "Then let's do it again."

It took another hour or so to lay the rest of the voice tracks. When Josie finally glanced at the clock, she wasn't surprised. 3:15 A.M. She'd been in the studio later than that before, sometimes until the early hours of the morning, leaving just in time to see the sun rise. But they'd made good time tonight. She was pleased with what they had accomplished and she could tell Brock was too.

"You'll have a good demo CD to shop around when this is done," she said, punching the stop button, then the rewind. "I'll have some rough CD's ready for you before you come in for tomorrow's session. We can make any changes tomorrow night."

"Wonderful." Brock just stared at her. She had a feeling he wasn't talking about the demo.

He followed her into the studio and began wrapping cords.

Startled, she said, "You don't have to do that. I can take care of all this."

"We'll get it done in half the time if we do it together." He finished wrapping a cord while she unhooked the microphone and brought it to the supply cabinet.

Her hands stopped mid-motion closing the door when he came over and leaned against the cabinet. "What is it?" she asked.

He bit his bottom lip. "Come with me."

Josie blinked. "What do you mean? Where are you going?"

"On the road. It'll be loads of fun."

She laughed, couldn't help herself. "I don't think so."

He gently gripped her by her upper arms, his face in a wide smile that made her heart stop.

"I need you, Josie. You're incredible. I've got some gigs lined up and some important people are coming out to see us. I don't want some part-time sound guy who doesn't know what I'm about doing my sound for me. That was fine when all I was doing was playing at the dance hall back in Steerage Rock. But this is important."

Still feeling the sensation of his hands on her, she sighed softly. Brock Gentry wasn't just some slick musician. He had the kind of talent that didn't come from years of practice or paying dues. It was just part of him. He was that good. She knew how important it was to get exposure and how annoying technical mistakes on the road, no matter how little, could make or break what might ultimately turn into a record contract.

She also knew she wasn't going to go on the road again. Not ever.

Blue suit. Blue suit, she muttered to herself for a full thirty seconds as she played tug of war with the idea in her head.

"No, thank you. I'm done with the road." Josie moved to go past him, to just get some distance because somewhere deep down she recognized something dangerous building inside her. She wanted to go with Brock. The problem was she couldn't identify exactly why.

Was it because on some level she longed to be in that atmosphere again, among people who shared her love of music? Or was it the man himself that drew her toward packing her bags and leaving again? Either way, it was going to derail a path she'd been determined to stay on for the better part of four years.

Brock shifted, just enough to move closer to her, making it difficult for her to make a quick getaway. Her breath hitched as the scent of him drifted to her. He ran his hand gently up her arm, but didn't say anything.

He was completely male in all the ways she hadn't wanted to see, Josie realized. His musky cologne blended in with the scent of his skin, not overpowering it, but enhancing it. They were close enough so that she could smell the coffee on his breath and feel the heat of his body even though they weren't touching.

She'd lied to herself big time, thinking this was just another session and that Brock was just another musician.

"We're good together. I can feel it," he whispered after a moment.

She felt it too, although she'd rather chew her tongue off than admit it.

"What are you afraid of?" he asked, tilting her chin up with his fingers.

She wanted to laugh. There was plenty to be afraid of, not the least of which was Brock Gentry.

He's just a kid, she reminded herself. He doesn't know what's ahead of him on this road. He was looking at her all starry-eyed as if she was his one-way ticket to success.

She opened her eyes and looked directly into his. Yeah, she'd been lying to herself. Brock may be a few years younger than her, but he was a man, strong and determined, with a wild fire that right at that moment was sparking a flame so strong in her she could hardly breathe.

She pulled away and took a step aside.

"Look, I've been on the road before. It's fun for a while, you see new places, meet new people. But before long it all looks the same. You don't remember what city you're in or even what day of the week it is."

"It's Tuesday," he said with a smirk. "I can keep track of the days for you."

She shook her head when she realized he wasn't going to give up easily.

"I'm not looking for what you're asking," she said resolutely.

"You think you've seen it all. Is that it?"

"I've seen enough."

"You've never been on the road with me."

Then she laughed. What was this guy all about? "I don't need to."

She waved her hand toward him and started to pace, if only just to get a few more feet away from Brock and clear her head.

"I've seen a hundred bright-eyed country boys like you walk through that door this year alone. You're too green to know what's ahead of you and believe me that's okay. Ignorance is bliss in this business."

"What made you so cynical? Was it Grant Davies?"

Her insides fell. Her relationship with Grant had been discrete. He'd wanted it that way at first. Only those people in their close circle knew they'd been in love. She'd been in love, she reminded herself.

Sighing, she propped herself on the edge of the stool sitting next to the empty mike stand and bit her lip. "I'm no gypsy, Brock. I found that out a long time ago. I know going on the road would be fun. For a while, that is. But after a short time, it'll be just another place that's too far from home. I'm not your girl."

"I'm not looking for you to be anything more than my sound engineer."

Now he was the one lying. What's more, he knew she knew and still, Brock didn't do anything at all to hide that fact.

"I can't commit to anything. Going on the road

means leaving here and forgetting the plans I've been making."

"I'd like to hear about those plans. Maybe we can get out of here and find an all night diner, grab some breakfast."

She laughed, covering her face with both hands. "First dinner, now breakfast? You do move quickly, cowboy."

"Hesitate too long and you lose the moment." Brock stared at her for a lingering moment. "It's just some coffee, maybe steak and eggs to go with it or a bagel. You like bagels, don't you? It can't hurt. Besides, if you're so wed to the plans you've made, there isn't a thing I can say to you over breakfast to talk you out of them."

"I have to go home. Dexter's been alone for too long."

"Dexter?"

She wanted to avoid the discussion about how obviously pathetic her life seemed. Josie had to admit she'd loved every moment working on Brock's demo tape. It'd been a while since she'd been able to sink her teeth into anything other than fluff radio spots. Now that she'd stretched her arms and legs into a new place, she knew it was going to be hard to curl them back into her little box.

"He's my cat. He's old and ornery, but the love of my life. And don't you say anything smart about it," she said, pointing a finger at him.

He laughed, something rich and deep and . . . it did things to her. Darn, if her heart didn't flutter just a little.

"I wouldn't dare. Besides, I like animals. Had an ornery old farm dog myself. I've lived my whole life on a ranch in Steerage Rock. And as much as I'm sure Dexter's been missing you, I know he'll survive another hour or two while we share a bagel."

Josie was being ridiculous. She'd planned on being at the studio the whole night. Using Dexter as an excuse to flee from Brock Gentry was taking the coward's way out. "Who said anything about sharing?"

Brock's lips tilted to one side. "Okay, you can have your own. I'll help you lock up and then we can go."

Unlike Brock, Josie knew the places to go this late at night that served the best breakfast in this part of Texas. She'd been there before with Grant's band and then just with Grant. Something about tonight made all that come back to her. As they walked through the doors of the diner, it felt as if she'd been there just yesterday, but it had been many years since she'd taken on a late night session. She had to wonder if maybe she'd made a mistake in accepting this invitation.

Brock ordered them a couple of coffees while she blankly looked at the menu, not really reading it. She was hungry for something, but didn't see anything that jumped off the menu. She settled on an apple cinnamon muffin when the aroma from one the waitress was delivering to a nearby table reached her nose.

"So what's the real reason you won't go on the road with me?" he asked.

She lifted her face from the menu she still held in

front of her despite having made her selection. "Because I don't want to."

He smirked and shook his head. "Not good enough. I figured you for at least some wild, elaborate story about how your long lost uncle or somebody needed you to come back and work the family farm."

She sputtered. "Who'd ever give a lame reason like that?"

He rested his elbows on the table and leaned forward. "Actually, that's what happened to my sister-in-law, Mandy. Came back to Texas to help her uncle with his ranch and ended up falling in love all over again with my older brother, Beau. Been married now a couple of years."

"Well, ain't that sweet," she said, trying to sound sarcastic, but the envy of it all got the better of her. She'd become a sap in her adult life. Happily ever afters made her weepy and long for one herself.

"Yeah. I've got a pretty little niece named Promise. My little sweet pea. She likes to pull at the strings of my guitar when I'm playing. And they've got another one on the way now."

"I get it. So the house is getting crowded and it's time to pack up and go on the road? Is that your story?"

"You want to know my story, but I've already told you and I think you can pretty much figure on your own what I didn't tell you. It's pretty simple stuff, and I'm a simple man."

Josie doubted that. There was something very real and compelling about Brock Gentry. Words couldn't quite capture him. Not anything she could come up with anyway, and she'd tried over these last days to do just that. When she'd seen him walk into the studio that first time, she thought she knew him or at least his type. She'd been dead wrong.

"I want to know your story, Josie," he was saying as he played with the paper napkin, dipping it in the water ring on the Formica table and then twisting it as if he were ringing out a wet rag. "You tell me you don't want to go on the road. But I saw you in that studio. You love what you do. You were as lost in what we were doing as I was."

Josie couldn't deny it or push back the smile that pulled at her cheeks. She couldn't remember the last time she'd enjoyed working in the studio this much. There was room to grow here, to be challenged and find the creative energy that sparked her to life—things she wasn't likely to find taping dog food commercials.

And there was this man, who with every breath he took, intrigued her.

She wanted to go on the road again. Sure. But that wasn't going to happen. She'd been there, done that, as the saying went. She didn't need a repeat of her broken heart. She didn't need to be trampled by studio executives who only looked at the bottom dollar and not at the artist or his craft. People who molded, shaped, and dressed a person until you no longer recognized the man beneath all that flare.

It would happen to Brock. And that was a crying shame. The man had talent in every inch of his being. And the dogs of the recording industry would chew him to pieces.

Chapter Three

"**I**'ve got to be out of my mind," Josie said, stuffing an extra sweatshirt into her duffle bag. She owned a nice black leather set of luggage her mother had given her when she graduated high school. She'd only used it once. It was too nice to be thrown around in the bottom of a dusty bus cargo hatch, being crushed by equipment, or on the bus, getting food and drink spilled on it.

And she had to pack light. Space was limited when sharing quarters and before too long, she knew the nice little things she thought she needed on the road would only be in the way. One big bag was all she was taking. If she couldn't fit her needs in there, it wasn't coming on the road with her. She'd probably get enough ribbing from the band for the things she couldn't part with.

And then she'd give it right back. No matter how many trucks they had to haul their equipment, the bus would have a few instruments the musicians wouldn't leave in the equipment truck. A guitar was like a security blanket to a musician.

Yes, she was out of her mind, she decided as she pulled the hooded sweatshirt over her head.

"Don't look at me that way," she said, ignoring the penetrating gaze of her faithful feline friend. Judgment was harsh, swift, and always hurt when she saw the truth staring back at her. "This is an important career move. I'm not a naive girl who's fresh out of high school anymore. I've grown. I've learned from my mistakes."

A quick roll of his eyes, or maybe it was just a half-lidded, sleepy gaze—with Dexter, she never knew—and she found herself defending her decision even further. "I'm not going to get involved with the man. I'm just going to make some contacts, meet some people. Maybe by this time next year I'll be working in a Nashville recording studio with Garth Brooks!"

Or some other country singer. As long as it wasn't Grant Davies, it didn't really matter. There was a lot of talent out there. The more she'd thought about things as she fitfully tangled herself in her sheets last night, the more she'd come to realize she'd sold herself out for the likes of Grant Davies and a broken heart. She was playing it safe doing dog food commercials and audio books.

It had been her decision, of course. She couldn't blame him for everything. Only for the broken heart he'd left her with. And even then, there'd been signs she'd ignored.

But leaving her career behind? No, that was all her

doing. That and everything she'd done since. It was time to make a change, keep on stretching her legs.

"I've worked on my last dog food commercial, Dex," she said as she zipped her bag, happy the last of the things she'd need on the road were packed. "Come on, boy."

Josie carefully lifted Dexter into her arms and opened the small kennel door, closing the cage after she'd coaxed the cat inside. He'd only given her a marginal fight this time. He'll be happy to discover this trip didn't include a stop at the veterinarian's office. Until then, Josie knew she'd have to deal with his wails of distress in the car. Once they were on the road, he'd become acclimated to the bus and even come to like it.

"At least you'll be my one true friend on the road," she crooned at the eyes looking back at her from the cage. "Even though I'll be totally outnumbered."

She changed her mind at least one hundred times between the time she dropped her bag in the trunk of her car and drove the thirty-minute drive to where the band was meeting. All the while, Dex wailed and Josie wanted to wail with him.

What was she thinking? Didn't smart women learn from their mistakes?

"This isn't a mistake. It's a new direction. An adventure, Dex," she said to the cat as she pulled into the parking lot and saw the bus. "It's a chance for me to prove something to myself. For once I'm not going to run away like a dog with her tail tucked between her legs."

Dex gave a plaintive cry. Josie wasn't sure if it was

the reference to the dog or the fact that she'd just pulled up next to the big, touring bus. The engine was burning diesel, making noise and spewing choking, hot fumes. Dex meowed a little more as she opened the passenger side door and pulled him out by the handle of the animal carrier he was secure in.

"It's going to be okay, Dex. Remember, it's an adventure."

God, she hoped so. She hoped it wouldn't end up being an adventurous disaster.

"You made it," Brock said, coming out from around the front of the bus.

"Was there ever a doubt?" she quipped nervously.

He just smiled and reached out to take the carrier from her.

Josie shook her head. "Nope, not this one. This is precious cargo. He comes with me."

"I'll take your luggage then."

"I just have a duffle in the trunk, and some things to make Dexter comfortable."

"I still can't believe I let you talk me into taking a cat on the road."

"Where I go, Dex goes. No room for negotiations there. He travels well though. You'll hardly notice him at all. You see, it's a package deal with us."

His smile was like sunshine, warming her to the core. "It's a fine package."

Still, she rolled her eyes. "Can't you think of a better pickup line?"

He looked momentarily hurt, until the corners of his lips curled into a smile that lit his eyes. And he had the most extraordinary eyes.

"I'll have to remember that about you. Nothing halfway, nothing phony."

"Absolutely. Give me the real thing or nothing at all."

What the heck were they talking about? She wasn't in the market for anything from Brock other than a chance to do what she loved. This was a second chance to prove herself, and do things right. Dance with the big boys, rough it out with the mad dogs and come out a winner. A winner doing things her way for a change, instead of getting a dog food commercial bone thrown at her.

"I'll be sure to remember that about you." His smile returned and when it did something sparked to life deep in her soul. He had a nice smile, genuine and pleasing. Josie found it hard to turn away from him.

In the studio, Brock had been focused and passionate about what he was doing. Sure, there was ribbing all around by the musicians and sometimes it got out of hand when the locker room talk escalated. Then they'd all remember there was a woman in the room and that usually amounted to tossing cold water on the subject.

Josie had laughed a few times about the looks on their faces. She was used to the boys room talk and felt comfortable around it, even if she knew her presence wasn't always welcome. She did know that she belonged there, a part of it all.

And she belonged here, she decided as she boarded the bus. Something about this journey felt like going home.

Josie sat in the back of tour bus, quietly removed from the boisterous activity of the rest of the band as they argued about the set list. She seemed at home here, Brock thought with relief. Removed, but still very much a part of what was going on. That was good. He'd half expected her not to show up.

She had the cat on her lap and lovingly stroked his fur in long, tender strokes. Every so often, she'd gaze out the window and turn her head back to him. Their eyes would meet and she would smile. A simple gesture, but it was nothing short of splendid.

And something inside him did funny things. He couldn't quite put a finger on it or figure out what was drawing him toward her. Or making his mouth say the most idiotic things.

"Twenty-three cities in twenty-five days. Twenty-three shows in less than four weeks." Miles Roper, the drummer who'd worked with them in the studio and had only just starting working with Brock live, stood up, drumsticks between his fingers, and gestured to the other bands members as if he were about to pull a rabbit out of a hat. "Now whose bright idea was this?"

The sound of a tab from a soda can being popped cut through the hum of wheels rolling over the pavement. "What are you belly-aching about, Miles? You've got two days off," Brock's manager said, taking a sip from the can and then licking his lips.

"It's not the time off I'm worried about. It's being stuck on this bus with the likes of ole Roy, here. I know how foul smelling he is in the morning."

"Didn't I tell you? You're sharing a bunk with Roy," Will said laughing, thumbing toward the brawny six-foot-five bass player who was taking up the space of two people with arms and legs spread wide as he sat eating from a large bag of barbeque chips. Roy stopped eating long enough to blow a teasing kiss at Miles.

"Oh, Lord, I'm in trouble. Just don't eat anything with beans."

Brock laughed as he made his way to the back where Josie was sitting. She'd been quiet since they'd boarded the bus, but she'd been taking everything in. He'd been watching her.

As he dropped down beside her on the small seat, she rewarded him with a smile that made his mind play tricks on him. He never quite knew what the woman was thinking or what she was feeling behind those beautiful eyes.

She motioned to Will with her head as she continued to stroke the cat's fur.

"So what's the deal with Will? How'd you meet him?"

Brock glanced over at Will, who was still giving a good teasing to Miles since he was off the phone. In a way, it felt strange to be going on the road with people he'd hardly known three months ago. Of all of them, he knew his manager the best.

"Will Harlen scooped me up out of nowhere less than a year ago after seeing me play a solo impromptu gig outside Steerage Rock."

Her eyebrows rose. "You were playing without a band?"

"I hooked up with these guys after I met Will. You could call it fate. I hadn't even been scheduled to play that night. Will had come down from Houston to see another country band he'd heard about. I was only there that night to see them."

"How'd you end up on stage?"

A tractor-trailer whizzed past the bus, momentarily drawing their attention out the window. When Brock turned back to Josie, her attention was fully on him.

"The drummer came down with an untimely case of the stomach flu."

"Oh, no."

"Yep. The rest of the band wanted to go on with the show, but having their drummer puking his brains out wasn't going to make it happen."

Josie giggled and covered her mouth with her hand. "That's awful."

"Yeah, it was a tough break for them since Will was there to see them. I didn't even know who he was, just heard some people talking about he'd come down to our neck of the woods in search of the next Grant Davies."

She flinched only slightly with the mention of Grant's name and then recovered.

"Isn't that what everyone wants these days? Another Grant Davies?"

"His music has been playing on all of the country stations. He's touring and making money for the record label that had scooped him up a few years back and everyone wanted to emulate the kind of success the man has achieved."

"Is that what you want?"

"I told you. I prefer his earlier work."

She smiled at that, something warm and kind and he forced himself not to reach out and touch her face.

"That you did."

She turned to look out the window again, her hand still poised on Dexter's back. Through the rumble of the bus, Brock could still hear the cat's purr. Yeah, something was purring in him these days and he knew it had a lot to do with this woman.

"Finish your story," she said.

He shrugged. "I spotted Will and he was looking really bored and impatient like he was ready to leave. I figured it was my open window."

Brock thought back to that night and how it had turned a small town country boy into something that people were starting to talk about. He'd heard the rumor that Will Harlen had connections in Nashville. He could make things happen. And he was there that night for a band that didn't stand a chance of even stepping on the stage to show what it could do.

Brock had known how to spot a window of opportunity. To have not made a move would have been like banging on a locked door when there was a perfectly good window to sail through. He was no fool.

"Management was getting a little antsy about losing their drinking crowd so I offered to step onto the stage and do a solo set to keep the crowd happy. At least until the headlining act got his head out of the toilet. All things considered, management offered me the stage. I'd never played a live show solo before. There was comfort in having some familiar faces on stage with me, even if I was the only one singing. But luckily, I managed to get Will's attention."

Of course, it almost hadn't happened. Brock recalled how when he'd stepped onto the stage and the spotlight hit his face, blinding him, he thought for one brief moment that he was about to join the drummer in the john. But luckily, the moment quickly passed, and the fear ebbed to something exciting instead of something driving his nerves to shreds. And just seconds after he'd announced himself and taken that first strum on the guitar he'd borrowed from the other band, he could hear the silence of the room like the beat of a drum.

When the set was over and he'd stepped off the stage amidst a roaring crowd and headed to the bar for something to drink, the interest in Will Harlen's face was unmistakable. Will had bought him the drink that night and said, "Kid, I'm going to make you a star."

Normally Brock would have just shrugged it off. He lived in the real world where stars were in the sky and people were just people. But he'd been riding the high of that show, still feeling the adulation of the crowd and his own satisfaction. When Will said the words they'd sounded like music to his ears and like a kid wanting to believe in Santa, Brock wanted to believe him.

He sighed, bringing his thoughts back to the present. Twenty-three cities in twenty-five days.

"He's not the only eye you caught," Josie said, burrowing into his thoughts.

"We've got a short time to shape you all into a tight band," Will was saying as he poured over some paperwork. Pulling his cell phone out of his jacket pocket, he punched a number in with his thumb. "Twenty-three cities in twenty-five days is the best way to do that. The first few shows will be small. You're already getting the feel of each other like newlyweds. Three weeks from now—"

His call must have connected because Will was now totally focused on the conversation he was having with the person on the other end of the line. Brock had no doubt Will was making sure things happened.

He was going to be a star, Josie thought as she stroked Dexter's back. There was no doubt in her mind. He'd caught her eye as fast and sharp as Will's, but for a different reason.

Brock stood apart from the rest of the boys on the bus. She stood apart from all of them. But Brock was definitely something to look at. He shined like a new copper penny.

It wasn't glitz and glamour. Sure, he was handsome with his angular jaw and the authentic cowboy look. He cleaned up better than most men she'd ever met in her life. But it was more than that. There was nothing phony about Brock Gentry. He wasn't hotheaded or impulsive. He thought before he spoke, and truly meant the things he said. And everybody listened to him.

Brock pulled himself up from the seat beside hers and moved toward the front where he stood in the aisle, listening to whatever Will was saying to the other person on the phone, taking it all in. He seemed oblivious to how the other band members saw him.

He was different all right. And he definitely was not wearing a blue suit.

Josie sighed as she glanced out at the passing scenery, seeing but not really taking it all in. Dex seemed comfortable on her lap, warming her with his body and his companionship. The world would be an easier place if a woman only felt the need to fall in love with her cat, not a man.

Startled by the thought she jerked her head back to

Brock. The heat of a blush crept up her cheeks, burning them. As easy as it would be, she wouldn't fall in love with Brock Gentry. He had a way of making a girl feel starstruck with a single glance, a mere hint of a smile. Just having him sit here beside her had made her heart feel all girlish and giddy in a way she'd sworn she'd grown out of back in high school.

And yet, his way was so comfortable that he put her right at ease. There was no pretense, no competition.

She must have tensed because suddenly the cat leaped from her lap and ran to the back of the bus, climbing onto one of the bunks. Josie had sworn that even though she insisted Dexter come with them on the tour, she wouldn't let her cat intrude on anyone else's space. It was only fair. Dex was *her* security, like a warm blanket and an old friend, no one else's.

Holding on to the wall, she made her way to the back of the bus where the bunks were. She found Dex on a top bunk, settling in at the foot of the newly made bed.

"Not here, Dex," she said, lifting the cat off the comforter, his body growing long as he hung from her arm. "This is where we're sleeping for the next month."

She placed the cat in her bunk and moved the crate to her pillow. "Space is sparse, so don't go taking more than what's yours," she whispered.

"If that cat starts talking back to you, I'm out of here," Brock said from behind, his voice deep.

Josie swung around and found him right next to her. He held the cabinet above to keep himself steady as the bus merged into the next lane and just looked at her. He had magnificent blond hair. Even the crease marks left by his cowboy hat were appealing to Josie and had her fingers itching to comb through them to make them smooth again. And she had no doubt his hair was soft as silk to the touch.

She was in trouble.

"Blue suit," she muttered with a sigh, turning away and moving toward the back of the bus. She needed the space from Brock and on this bus that was going to be hard to manage. As she moved down the aisle past the other bunks, she spied the bathroom and realized that was the only place to which she could retreat.

By the sound of his boots hitting the floor, she knew Brock had followed her. She was trapped.

"I can wait if you need to go first," she said, turning around and gazing up at him.

The engine noise was louder in the back of the bus, although it may simply be that the talk and music playing in the front drowned out the sound.

"Is that why you really came back here?" he said, his voice low and thick.

She almost laughed. Not because they were standing there on a bus rolling down the interstate, making small talk about who should go to the bathroom first, but because she'd clearly given herself away.

But she held her composure in check. Josie was good at that. She could easily hold her distaste for someone else's music out of kindness as well as she could hold her emotions in check. Grant had accused her of staying too reserved. But stroking someone's ego just for the benefit of building oneself up wasn't her style. Had never been. Somehow, though, she'd slipped and Brock must have seen the thoughts that had been rolling around in her mind.

Someone in the front of the bus laughed loudly, making Brock turn around for a second. Josie used that moment to collect her thoughts.

"Hey, if you've got a better reason than using the bathroom, go for it. I just figured I'd be polite."

"What does 'blue suit' mean?" he asked, ignoring her lame attempt at changing the subject.

Darn! She knew she'd grimaced when Brock's lips went askew in a knowing expression.

"Blue suit?"

"Don't play dumb with me. The first time you said it in the studio, I figured I was hearing you wrong and you must have been talking to yourself about something. But this is the third time I've heard you say that. Blue suit. And always right before you turn on your heels and hightail it in the other direction. I figure I must be doing something to cause this. I just don't know what it means."

Closing her eyes, Josie leaned against the back wall and considered lying. It would be easy. But this was going to be a long road trip if the lies started here. They'd only get bigger and longer and harder to manage, not to mention leave a bitter taste in her mouth for doing it. All just to keep the man from knowing what he already suspected—that she was wildly attracted to him.

"That's what I'm going to marry." Opening her eyes, she stuck out her chin and looked up at Brock. His expression was blank.

"You're going to marry a blue suit?"

She forced a smile. She knew it sounded ridiculous, even to her own ears. But it was a decision she'd made long ago, a planned path she'd managed to derail from when Grant Davies had entered her life. One she was determined to stay on now no matter how attracted she was to Brock Gentry.

"It's just a figure of speech. I don't want a man who is never around. I want to marry someone with a normal job and a normal life. Someone who gets up every morning and comes home to me and me alone every night."

His eyebrows creased. "Most people look for a person they can love, not the clothes they wear."

"Ah, but that's where you're wrong," she said, standing up straighter. "People look at the outer package all the time. You can't say that these ads with stick-thin super models are meant for us to see their inner beauty. No, it's the package. The inner stuff comes later."

"How are you ever going to get to the inner stuff if all you're doing is looking at a man's job?"

Brock had a full-blown smile now. One that showed how completely adorable that lone dimple on his right cheek could make him. He was making fun of her and because she knew she sounded crazy, she couldn't help the heat that seared her cheeks.

"Okay, I know it sounds nuts. I'll admit that. But you don't have to agree with my ways."

He chuckled low and put his arm against the wall as she started toward him, preventing her from passing. "It's not a matter of agreeing. I just don't see how it's possible."

"How do you figure that? I'm pretty determined when I put my mind to something."

"I have no doubt about that. But I doubt very much that that heart of yours is looking for a boring man in a blue suit."

She straightened her spine and laughed hotly. "Who said anything about boring?"

"If all you're looking at is a man's occupation, how can it not be?"

"Lots of women hope to marry lawyers and doctors. I don't care what the man does so long as it's a job that's not going to take him on the road away from me."

Feeling the walls close in, Josie took another step forward, but Brock remained in place. One more step and she'd be on top of him. And with that thought, her imagination started to reel. He smelled too good, not just the light hint of cologne, but also the smell of clean soap and fresh air. She didn't want to look up at him, knowing her thoughts would betray her.

She'd made a colossal mistake in coming on this road trip. There was absolutely no way she could spend all her time in close quarters with Brock Gentry and not have him know how attracted to him she was. And if he could see it, then it was a safe bet the rest of the band could see it too. She didn't relish the idea of being the butt of every joke, hearing the snickers at her back or whispers when she entered the room.

"So what does that mean? No traveling salesmen?" He reached up and brushed his finger down her cheek and her head spun. "No musicians?"

"Please let me pass," she said, her voice failing her and coming out in a breathless plea.

"Why?" he said, tilting her chin up with his fingers. "So you can find your boring blue suit man? I don't think so."

"And why not?"

His eyes were magnificent and Josie could only

imagine how easy it would be to drown in them forever and not care about anything else. But she did care.

"You need a man who's not going to tie you down,
Josie."

"And you think you're so sure you know what I
need?"

He bent his head and brushed his lips against hers in
a kiss that was light as the breeze. His hot breath teased
her skin and made her head float. She closed her eyes
and against her better judgment, she fell against his
chest and into the kiss he offered. He wasn't demanding, not at first anyway, and for that brief moment, Josie
forgot about all the reasons why she shouldn't be kissing Brock and focused on all the reasons why she
should.

He pulled away and through her dazed eyes, she saw
he was smiling down at her, his lips full and moist from
their kiss.

"You're kidding yourself big time. You've got a
gypsy heart, lady. No blue suit man is going to change
that."

Chapter Four

"Don't do that again," she said, her eyes flaring in a way Brock had never seen before. The little flecks of gold in her eyes sparked to life and seem to glow like burning embers. Brock was tempted to test her, see how far he could push her until the slow burning embers came to a roaring flame. Not one to push a woman beyond her comfort zone, however, he held himself back and followed her lead.

If she was feeling even half of what he was feeling after that kiss . . . Holy smokes!

"Why not?" he asked, trying not to smile because he knew it would only irritate her. And right now, Josie was fired up as hot as the engine moving them down the highway. "I thought it was kinda nice."

That was putting it mildly. His body was still feeling the effects of holding Josie in his arms. His mouth could still taste her, but Brock didn't elaborate further. There were too many eyes on his back as it was and he didn't want to risk making her feel uncomfortable in front of everyone and having no place for her to retreat.

"That's not the point," she said, glancing past him to the front of the bus.

He could have sworn he caught her lips trembling and his mind reeled with the memory of having his mouth on hers just moments ago, how it completely rattled him. He thought of what it would be like to kiss Josie on many occasions. His imagination paled to reality. "Then what is it?"

She laughed, touching her forehead with her hand and darting her gaze up front again, then back at his face. "I should think it would be obvious."

"Maybe to you."

"I have to live on this bus for the next month under the watchful eyes of all of them." Sighing, she pointed to the front of the bus.

Brock glanced over his shoulder, but thankfully everyone seemed to be oblivious to the two of them. Miles and Roy had moved on from sleeping arrangements and were now arguing over which fast food restaurant had the best french fries. Will was on the phone again, no doubt talking rings around whoever was on the other end. Matt was sitting upright, sound asleep on the sofa.

"There is no reason for us to keep this secret," he said, reaching his hand out to touch her hair. He'd thought of doing this at least a hundred times while he'd been alone with Josie in the studio. But he didn't dare. In the studio, he remained professional, keeping his mind on the work they had to do. That didn't mean he hadn't thought of her endlessly or about how it would feel to tangle his fingers in her dark hair and kiss her like he'd just done. Her hair was thick and silky, much like he'd imagined. A smile rose up inside him with the discovery.

Josie shook her head, pulling back from his reach. "Believe me, it wouldn't even work to try and keep it a secret. Nothing we do will be a secret for long while we're living in such close quarters. Please, Brock. What just happened was a mistake. It can't ever happen again."

In her eyes, he saw that she was unsure, maybe even as rattled by their kiss as he was. That was a good thing because he didn't want to think that what he'd been feeling these last few weeks was all one-sided. He'd imagined Josie feeling those same things too.

There were times when he'd look at Josie and would think they were both talking to each other, saying the same things with their eyes. Only with their eyes. When his lips had touched hers just now, he knew her response, understood it, even though she was trying to deny it now. She was good at pulling back her emotions. He already had that part of her figured out. He just didn't know why.

"Brock, it was a mistake," she repeated in a rushed whisper.

He shook his head and reached for her, brushing his hand along her hair and settling it on her shoulder. Something warm and tingling stirred inside him with the contact. He was infinitely glad that Josie didn't pull away.

"You're telling me you didn't feel a thing? Nothing at all?"

She lifted her chin in challenge but didn't say a word.

He sighed. "Okay. Are you telling me that what's been happening between us is all in my head? If the answer is yes, then I'll leave you alone. I won't touch you again and we can forget this ever happened."

Josie gazed up at him with those unbelievably beautiful eyes. His mouth suddenly went cotton dry and the air around him seemed to be sucked right out of his lungs as he waited for her answer.

"No." She glanced at the ground for a brief second and shook her head. Brock was comforted in knowing she hadn't lied to him about her feelings. It made him that much more determined to figure out what she was so afraid of. Tipping her chin up with his fingers, he forced her to look him in the face.

"Good. I was afraid this *was* all in my head."

Bending his head to kiss her again, he was startled and a little disappointed as she pulled back.

"We have an audience."

He chuckled low, shock replaced by a light heart.

"I didn't figure you for being shy. Is that what's bothering you?"

"I can't believe it doesn't bother you."

Brock shrugged and moved in closer to her, mere inches from her ear. "It shouldn't be a problem. It just means we're going to have to be a little creative if we want to steal a few minutes alone."

Sighing, Josie crossed her arms over her chest. "It's more complicated than that and you know it. Twenty-three cities in twenty-five days. Every waking moment is going to be spent living and breathing the next show."

Josie shook her head, biting on her bottom lip. "This isn't the right time. We can't do this."

"We can, if we both want it."

"Every conversation we have comes back to the band, or recording, or the show. What do we have outside of this? We don't know each other outside the band and what we do here."

"Twenty-three cities in twenty-five days. We've got the time to get to know each other, Josie. I want to know all the reasons why you're looking for a blue suit. I want to know your favorite color, flavor of ice cream, and why you lobbied so hard to get your cat a seat on this bus."

"I told you. It may sound crazy, but I don't go anywhere without Dex."

"It means you're a loyal friend. I like that. That's a good quality."

"Is that what you want out of this? A friend?" she asked, cocking her head to one side. "Just for the record, I'm not in the habit of passionately kissing my friends."

The sound of boots coming closer had Josie glancing over his shoulder and caused Brock to turn as well. Will was treading down the aisle toward them.

"The next stop is in about a half hour. We can all stretch out our legs a bit," Will said. "I just set up a photo gig. We've got to get you some shine, kid. These clothes are the pits."

Running a hand down the front of his chest, Brock said, "What's wrong with what I have?"

Will chuckled. "Boy, you look like you just walked right off the pasture. You need some flash. Something that's going to make people notice you. Trust me on this. People are going to remember the name Brock Gentry."

"They're going to remember me, all right," Brock said, standing in front of the tri-fold mirrors at the department store. "I look like a Christmas tree bulb. I can't wear this."

He started unfastening buttons, but Will moved in front of him and stopped him.

"You look great, kid," Will said, giving him a slap on the back. "They're going to love you."

Irritation clouded Brock's face. "I want to get out of this getup."

Josie wanted to puke. She had to agree with Brock's assessment of himself. The red satin cowboy shirt was a far cry from his normal attire of a simple black cotton T-shirt and jeans. The colored boots matched the jewel-studded jeans. Flashy, yes. But it wasn't Brock. Or rather, it wasn't the Brock she'd come to know.

"I'm not wearing this on stage. I don't even recognize me." Brock laughed, but Josie could tell there was no humor behind it. He pulled at the collar of the shirt and at the waist where he wore a wide buckle.

The tailor came out from the back room with a small sewing box and began pushing Brock's arms up to make him look as if he were about to take flight. Pulling at the red satin fabric, he stuck pins in here and there and proclaimed himself finished.

"The clothes will be ready in an hour. Why don't you get a bite to eat while I finish up?"

"Sounds like a good plan. We need to top it off though," Will said, pulling the tailor away before turning back to Brock. "Don't get out of that shirt just yet. I want you to try on a few hats."

Why Josie was sitting there witnessing this, she wasn't sure. Brock had asked her to come along proclaiming he might need a woman's touch. There wasn't a whole lot for her to do on the road when he wasn't performing. And as much as she loved her cat, Dex was more than willing to be left on his own for hours on end. So she'd come along to observe, but gave little in the way of encouragement when Will insisted on Brock trying on all those gaudy clothes.

Brock glanced at her through his reflection in the mirror. "What do you think?"

Should she tell him? "Depends on what kind of look you're going for."

He sputtered. "Not this one."

"Then tell Will."

"You heard me. He seems to think this is going to give me an image."

"I like the one you had," she said softly, smiling at his reflection.

I'm not in the habit of passionately kissing my friends. Had she really said that to him? Could she have been any more obvious? They weren't more than a day into this road trip and she'd already kissed the man—passionately, in the back of the bus. Oh, God!

Her comment seemed to please him, relaxing his expression just a bit. "I don't want to be just friends, Josie," he said quietly. There was no one else around them in the store and yet Josie still felt as if all eyes were on them.

Will's sudden approach with an armful of cowboy hats kept her from having to answer. Plopping a matching hat on Brock's head, he said, "This is the one."

Brock groaned.

With a roll of her eyes, Josie said, "I'll meet you outside."

She waited for Brock to go into the dressing room and then turned toward the door.

"He's something else, isn't he?" Will said, walking along by her side.

"Sure is," Josie answered, but she was sure Will saw Brock in a different light than she did.

Although she had to admire Will for his accomplishments and for what he was trying to do for Brock, the man knew a meal ticket when he saw it and Brock was surely going to make him fat. She didn't think there was a person among them that didn't believe the course they were on wouldn't lead to a major recording contract. She wasn't sure she agreed with his style or his vision for Brock, but it wasn't up to her to voice her opinion with Will.

That was for Brock to do. She had a feeling she'd be hearing him voice it loudly if Will kept up his pushing.

"He's a good kid," Will said, putting his arm around Josie's shoulder. "It would be a shame for him if his priorities got a little clouded."

Josie shot Will a sidelong glance. "Brock seems pretty sure of himself. He'll do just fine."

"It would help if you had given him a little more encouragement back there."

"I'm not going to lie, Will, and Brock can come to his own conclusions without my help."

He gave her a hard, cold look as they reached the clothing store door. Josie put her hands on the metal bar to push to the outside, but Will caught her upper arm. "Are you sure about that?"

"What is that supposed to mean?"

"I've seen the way he looks at you. You've been on the road. You know how it works. It's important for Brock to play to the crowd and that means the women too. Is that something you can handle?"

Annoyance rose up like bile in her throat. She pulled her arm from his grip. "You don't really care what I can handle, Will. You and I both know that. You just want to make sure I stick around and play nice until we reach Nashville."

He laughed, but there was an edge to his voice that held a warning. "This is important."

"I know." It was important to both of them.

"I can't have him losing confidence because of how starry-eyed he gets around you. I went along with his insistence that you work in the studio with him and it worked out just fine. We got a fine demo. But I don't want to lose sight of what the goal is here."

"That's not going to happen."

Will was right. She knew how it was on the road with a band. She'd been there before. Josie wasn't going to do something as stupid as make a scene if an over-zealous new fan ran up to Brock and gave him a kiss. She didn't come on this road trip to find a boyfriend or a musician to marry. There'd be plenty of time for finding a solid relationship once she'd settled in Nashville. And when she did, it wouldn't be with a music man.

No. Sweet kisses and warm embraces didn't only come from musicians. No matter how much the kiss she'd shared with Brock had stirred her soul, she wouldn't let it go that far between them.

"I just wanted to make sure we understand each other, Josie. Brock wants you here and that's why you're here." The implications of Will's words didn't escape her and pulled an old wound open, stinging.

"You've got your agenda, Will, and I have mine. Let's just leave things like that."

Josie pushed out the door and left Will to stare at her back as she made her way to the bus. She wasn't about to let him get the best of her even though her pulse hammered at her temple and her head felt as if it was about to blow sky high.

She was here because Brock wanted her here. In Will's mind, it wasn't her ability or that Brock saw something in her skills as a sound engineer that he wanted for his music. To Will, Josie was Brock's girlfriend and in the way of everything he'd been putting in place for his rising star.

When would it ever not be an uphill battle for her to be seen for what she could contribute and not just an add-on because the star performer had the hots for her?

Old wounds were always hard to close, but Josie tried as she took her first step up the stairs of the bus. As soon as she did, she immediately wanted to turn around and run back out to the sidewalk.

Today was the day for confrontations. Raised voices

in the back of the bus spelled trouble. But Dexter was also back there. He didn't like confrontations and usually hid with loud noise. She couldn't leave him alone in the middle of an argument with people he hardly knew.

Miles and Roy were arguing where Josie and Brock had been earlier. Where they'd both been standing when Brock had kissed her. What they'd shared was heated, but not the same as what was happening now.

"I turned my back for a second to pay the check and you moved in to score," Roy was saying, pointing a burly finger at Miles' chest.

"She was interested in me, anyway."

Roy huffed. "No way. You're a pity date."

"Oh, give it a rest, guys," Josie said wryly, reaching down to retrieve Dex, who'd curled up in a ball at the end of her bunk. She nuzzled the cat to her face. "Don't tell me you're already fighting over a girl."

"Stay out of this, Josie," Miles warned.

"This is going to be an agonizingly long trip if we're going to have to hear you two go at it every time you see a pretty face. Trust me, there'll be plenty more at the next stop."

For all of them. Including Brock, she thought, a sinking feeling dragging her mood even lower than it had been in the store.

"He's just sore, is all."

"Your cat got hair all over my black jacket," Roy said, ignoring his argument and Miles' comment. He picked up the jacket and thrust it at Josie.

"I'm sorry. I should have kept him in the crate while

I was in the store," she said, heat creeping up her cheeks. "Dexter doesn't know his boundaries yet."

Roy laughed wryly. "Yeah, I guess none of us do." He started toward the front of the bus and Josie called after him.

"I'll take care of the cat hair, Roy. I promise it won't happen again."

Roy waved a hand back at her. "Yeah, whatever."

She eyed Dexter, pulling up his face gently with her hand so she could look at him. "You're going to get us both thrown off this bus. You know better than to nap on someone else's bunk," she crooned. "I don't want to have to keep you kenneled in Nashville for the whole month until we can find someplace permanent."

Since the tailor finished Brock's new clothes faster than expected, they all ordered Chinese takeout for dinner. The rest of the band climbed aboard the bus and even though Will insisted they were ahead of schedule, he still wanted to get on the road. Unlike the first leg of their trip, the atmosphere on the bus had become strained while they dished out their food.

"What's chewing them?" Brock asked quietly, taking the seat opposite her at the dining table.

Josie took a sip of her soda. "Girl troubles."

Brock laughed. "That didn't take long."

Josie stared at him. Maybe she didn't find it as amusing as Brock because she herself felt some turmoil about what was happening between them. And she didn't really want anything to be happening between them that didn't have to do with her job as a sound engineer.

But it was undeniably there. Like right now as Brock's eyes lifted to hers from across the table. In his eyes, she saw the kiss, and Lord help her, she could feel it all over again.

The brief kiss they'd shared earlier had started something. No doubt about that. But if she was going to be honest with herself, then she had to at least admit there'd been something brewing right from the start, from the moment Brock had walked through the DB Sound Studio doors.

But it had to end here and now.

"Listen," she started, glancing around to make sure no one was focusing his attention on the two of them. She took his hand from across the table. "About what happened earlier today."

Brock's smile was immediate and the light in his eyes burst to life, making her heart flutter.

"It was really nice."

Josie couldn't deny that. Brock Gentry certainly wasn't the first man she'd ever kissed, but there was something about kissing him, his strength, and the way he made her head spin that had made her think it would be just fine if he were the last man she ever kissed.

"I could get used to having you in my arms like that."

She could get used to being held in his arms, feeling things she hadn't allowed herself to feel for any man in a long time. Closing her eyes to the images flooding her mind, she sighed.

"I hope you don't take this personally, but I meant what I said earlier. I don't want us to get involved with each other."

Some of the sparkle vanished from his eyes. "I thought we went through that already."

She nodded, pulled her hand away and picked up her fork, poking at her fried rice. "We're working together and things could get really complicated. I don't want anything to get in the way of us working together. You know what I mean?"

"Lots of musicians work together and have happy relationships. Look at Paul and Linda McCartney."

"Good try. But they were married before they began performing together and had a family they took on the road with them. Being around everyone while trying to start a relationship isn't my idea of romance."

"It could be. We could get out of here," he said, the smile on his face breaking her heart.

"Yeah—you, me, and the rest of the guys. I think I'll pass."

His brow crinkled. "Why do you do that?"

"I'm not doing anything but declining your offer."

"You're pushing me away."

"Is that a crime?"

"If you do it for the wrong reason, yes. I enjoy your company. I think you feel the same, but every time we get the tiniest bit close to each other and start to move to a new level, you either hightail in the opposite direction or push me away."

Sighing, she dropped her fork on the table again. She wasn't all that hungry anymore. "It isn't personal."

Brock laughed sarcastically. "So you say."

"It's just . . ." she said, trying to think of the right words to explain and coming up empty.

"You're still looking for a blue suit. Maybe I should have that tailor find one instead of that flashy, God awful red thing Will insisted on having me buy."

She chuckled and felt some of the tension ease. "Christmas tree bulb, huh?"

"Shoot, I'm going to blind everyone in the front row at tonight's show." Brock shifted in his seat, clearly uncomfortable.

"Seriously," she said, clearing her throat.

He filled in the blanks she'd left with her silence. "You and I can have some time to ourselves. It doesn't have to be us and the band all the time. There's a whole lot more to me than just this."

"That's just it. When we're together, all we do is talk about the band and that's fine, except . . ."

"There's more to you. I understand that. And that's a part of you I want to get to know."

"Outside of this, I don't know how to be. What are we going to do, sneak off and then come home?"

"Are you afraid of what they'll say?"

"No, not really. I just don't relish the idea of being under a microscope. And we will be, you know."

"I have to admit I'm not all that fond of having eyes on me all the time—except yours, of course."

He laughed at the look she threw him. "You can do better than that, cowboy."

"Don't push me away and I'll try better. I like you, Josie. A lot."

"I like it when you say things like that better than when you're trying to impress me with your words or your songs."

He tilted an eyebrow. "Hey, you don't like my songs?"

She laughed. "That's not the point."

"I'll leave you alone, if that's what you want. I won't push you to do anything you don't want to do. The last thing I want is to make you uncomfortable."

She looked at Brock a long time, looked into the depths of his magnificent eyes and wondered how she could have ever thought he was too young for her. In years, maybe. But that was just a play of numbers. He had a wise soul and it showed in what he did. And in his beautiful eyes. It didn't seem strange to refer to them that way. She didn't think she'd ever met a man who didn't push his way on her. Brock was different.

But Brock was different from the kind of man she'd convinced herself she needed. She couldn't imagine him sitting behind a desk and filling out paperwork all day. Growing up on a ranch had given him a different perspective on life than she had. But she couldn't see him lasting forever on a ranch, herding cattle and stringing barbed wire fences, either.

"You don't make me uncomfortable," she said. "In fact, it's just the opposite."

"That's good."

"It's this situation that bothers me. But that's the way it is. It's not something we can change."

"Brock?" Will called from the front of the bus. Will gave a strong look to Josie and she knew he was thinking about their conversation at the department store. She wouldn't let Will or anyone else intimidate her. She'd done that before and crawled home to regret it.

Before Brock turned his attention to Will, he reached across the table and squeezed her hand. "We can if we try. I want to try, Josie."

She watched as he got up from the table and walked down the aisle toward Will. When she'd packed her bags for this road trip, she'd promised herself there'd be no regrets this time around. She didn't want to think that she'd ever regret her decision to come on the road with Brock or anything at all about the man.

But she had to stay true to her goal. The end of the road for her was Nashville. She had a lot of catching up to do. Looking at Brock, she knew they both hoped for wonderful things in Nashville, but their roads were sure to turn in different directions once they arrived. She was going to have to be careful not to take the wrong path again.

Chapter Five

 T he first week on the road had been met with a series
of mishaps that were quickly fixed so that the audience
was left unaware to enjoy the show. Unloading and setting up quickly and not getting in each other's way
while doing their jobs was getting easier after their
tenth show, Josie discovered.

All of the early shows had been small, held in local
clubs and large dancehalls that drew a regular crowd no
matter who the headlining band was on the sign outside. It was a good way to bring in new fans and get
exposure for Brock on the local radio stations. The new
CD was starting to get airplay and that set everyone's
spirits a little higher.

The sound check had become a routine for Josie.
They'd all fallen into a groove, having spent so much
time in close quarters on the bus. Such is life on the
road, but it wasn't without a downside. Tensions flared
and then dissipated, usually by Will, who, being on the

phone a good deal of the time, would scold whoever was making the ruckus.

But despite the little spats that went on backstage and on the bus, the band had become tight, not unlike a married couple who'd grown through their first year as newlyweds. They'd done well and survived the first leg of the tour, but the big test would come when they reached the coast.

The mood had change as the anticipation of their first big show in Galveston approached. Josie could almost hear it like a hum getting louder by the moment until it became a roar.

Will had high hopes for Galveston. He'd said that everything they'd done so far was solely leading up to this one gig. From then on, every gig they had would build on the last.

They pulled into the fairgrounds, located on one of Galveston's thirty-two miles of beach.

"Hey, this is us," Miles said, reaching over to the stereo sitting in the overhead compartment. He turned up the volume. Brock's voice filtered over the speakers.

"When did this happen?" Roy asked Will.

Will just smiled.

"Did you think it was magic? The guy's got connections," Miles said, smacking Roy with a music magazine.

Roy pointed a finger at Miles and chuckled. "Don't start with me again."

"Enough, already," Will said, getting up and moving to the front of the bus. "This bus isn't big enough for you two to get into another wrestling match."

"Hey, Miles is just sore because I managed to get him in a headlock."

Josie glanced over at Brock, who was reclining in his seat, seemingly lost in the song playing on the radio. His song.

She leaned over, rested her elbows on her knees, and said quietly, "Cool, huh? To hear it on the air for the first time."

But instead of the elation the other band members were enjoying at this milestone, Brock appeared guarded, almost critiquing the music as he had in the studio.

Josie giggled with excitement. Her work was on the radio again. And not some little fluff dog food commercial. It was music she'd worked on. It had been a long time coming.

"You know, you can ease up a little and just enjoy the moment. This is big."

As she sang along with the radio, he smiled at her, something warm, wonderful, and wide.

"I've been dreaming of this day for a long time," he said quietly. "I knew it would come. Now that it has, it almost doesn't seem real."

"You can pinch yourself if it helps, but it's real. Hey, Miles, turn it up a little louder," she called out.

Brock listened intently to the music, a slight smile playing on his face as his teeth clamped down on his lower lip. "I didn't expect it would feel this good."

She tilted an eyebrow. "You are allowed to enjoy it, you know."

Another smile split his face. This one bigger and more of what she'd expected. In an instant, he was on his feet, picking her up and spinning her around. "I've dreamed of this for a long time," he said again, his eyes twinkling down at her.

It felt great to be in Brock's arms again, Josie thought. It seemed much too long since he'd held her and kissed her. They'd been so busy, and so many eyes had been on them that there hadn't been any opportunities for stolen moments like this.

"Will talked to the station manager. He said they've been playing it the last three days and started getting calls about the show. It almost doesn't seem real."

Josie nodded. "If you've been getting a lot of airplay, then it should be a great turnout with people who are coming to see you. It'll be a good show."

"Hey, when we get settled at the fairgrounds, why don't we take off?" she said, surprising herself with her spontaneity. "We can check out the fairgrounds together."

His expression faltered. "Will's got some interviews lined up for me as soon as we get there. I don't think there'll be any time."

She nodded, forcing a smile to cover her disappointment.

"Another time then."

Much to Brock's disappointment, they both were quiet the rest of the ride. As the bus rolled to a stop just outside the staging area, he saw the mob. Reporters and photographers wearing large VIP passes were already assembled by the gate, waiting to get a story. Will had indeed outdone himself this time. Smiling, Will climbed off the bus to greet the crowd, then gestured inside. Brock had no doubt he was making promises with his time to meet with each and every one of them.

"Looks like I'm on," he said to Josie, the pit of his stomach burning as he stared outside the tinted window. He was glad they couldn't see him or the apprehension that suddenly clutched him, leaving him weak.

Josie touched his hand and said, "Knock 'em dead." Her smile, the gentle touch of her hand giving him confidence broke the spell that had consumed him just moments earlier. He smiled and felt his fear turn to excitement.

This was it. He had their attention. It was time to give them what they wanted.

He squeezed Josie's hand and brought it to his mouth for a kiss before walking off the bus into the mayhem.

There had to be a hundred thousand people gathered for the two-day summer festival, Brock thought as he peered out the bus window. Few of the people who were eager to come to the festival had heard of Brock Gentry, but that didn't seem to matter to any of them. The number of people all gathered at the same time and the television footage of the outdoor concert with several other bands was what Will had said was going to set the stage for them to make the rest of the trip to Nashville.

They needed to make a big splash in Galveston and then continue on their way to Nashville riding on the success of the show. Brock watched from the back of the bus while Will worked the crowd of reporters. It was a good plan. Why was he so apprehensive?

Since they'd arrived at the parking lot of the fairgrounds, Will had been pulling him from one stop to the next interview, and to yet another photography session until Brock didn't even know which way was up.

Finally he was alone to enjoy his down time, the short hour he'd begged off to take a nap or to simply regroup on his own. He had come to value the privacy that was so rare on the road.

The rest of the band had taken this time to sightsee, as Josie had suggested they both do together when they arrived. Brock was grateful he didn't have to hear another petty squabble between Miles and Roy, or the phone ring and Will offering him up for another appearance for some radio show. The DJ's he'd met didn't have a clue who he was or what he was about. His excitement over doing the radio spot soon waned when he felt their lack of enthusiasm or had to answer the same question over and over, or listen to another lame joke about his new clothes.

Brock sighed as frustration made its way up his spine. He put his guitar down, placing it into the case and snapping the locks shut. He always wrote his songs in private. That's when his thoughts were his own and the noise of the world didn't intrude. But none of his thoughts were on his music now.

Dexter meowed as he prowled along the edge of Josie's bunk and made his way up to the front of the bus where Brock was reclining on the sofa. The cat rubbed his face against Brock's leg in a gesture of friendship. Without any thought, Brock obliged the cat by stroking its fur.

"You miss her, don't you boy?" he said quietly. Dexter lifted his head and gave a plaintive cry, as if he really knew Brock was talking about Josie.

"I miss her too." Sighing, he closed his eyes and leaned back against the cushion. There'd been no time for them at all, even though his mind always seemed to wander to Josie. There was a lot of idle time on the bus, even at the gigs, but never time alone. Today would have been a good day for them to connect. He was beginning to see why Josie felt a relationship between them wouldn't work on the road.

She'd calmed his nerves with a simple squeeze of the hand and a warm smile. In all his life, the only thing that had ever eased his anxiety was playing his guitar. It wasn't always possible to do that here on the bus, especially when he was never alone. But a simple touch from Josie's hand had done the trick when he felt his heart starting to race and his palms sweating. He'd been able to face the reporters when all he'd wanted to do was hide from their flashbulbs and barrage of questions.

But there was never time alone. No time for them to connect on any level other than business.

Unfettered, Brock stood up, walked to the kitchenette, and pulled open the refrigerator door. Grabbing the carton of milk, he poured himself half a glass and put an inch of milk in a plastic cereal bowl, offering it to Dexter. The cat immediately jumped to the counter and began lapping up the milk.

"This will be our little secret, okay?" he said with a chuckle, recalling how Josie had worked overtime to make sure the cat didn't jump on either the dining table or the counters. He stroked the cat's long, silky back and felt an ache in his heart that rose up and choked him.

Brock missed Josie. She'd been here on this bus the whole time, sleeping in a bunk not far from his, looking at him from beyond the spotlights every night as he sang, yet she felt far away, so unreachable. She'd kept an emotional distance from him ever since he'd reached for her and kissed her that first day.

What an idiot he'd been.

Somewhere in the back of his brain, he knew there'd be girls hanging about at every stop, after every performance. Miles and Roy were in seventh heaven. And Brock had to agree that Josie had been right about their every move being watched. He'd felt the stares at his back whenever they'd talk. He hated the feeling that he couldn't just reach for her again and let her know what he'd been feeling. He didn't want those other girls. He wanted her.

That empty ache in his gut began to grow and burn. He'd lived in a house as big as Texas growing up, but he'd always felt alone. His brothers were much older than him and had their own lives to live. As much as he knew they loved him, they'd never been close. He'd always been on his own and for most of his life, that had been fine with Brock.

He wasn't so sure anymore. Meeting Josie had changed that. He couldn't ever remember feeling the way she made him feel. It wasn't the words she said, it was the way she looked at him, saw through him like no one had ever done before. Certainly not like the girls who were always pulling at him and trying to steal a kiss or a hug after a show. Josie was different. And right now, he missed her more than he could handle.

Voices outside the bus made him groan. The band was on its way back. Roy and Miles were arguing about something else. It didn't matter if it was a woman or who took the last potato chip from the bag, they just loved to argue with each other. It reminded him a little bit of his brothers, Beau and Cody, who always seemed to be at the other's throat about something. A longing for home and that familiarity stabbed him.

With a sigh, he peered out the tinted windows and let his eyes graze the group to see if Josie was among them. He'd hoped she'd be here when he'd gotten back to the bus earlier. But he couldn't expect her to stay alone and be available just when he had time. It wasn't fair to ask her to hang around waiting for him either, when she could easily have a good time sightseeing with the other members of the band. He scanned the group heading toward the bus. Josie wasn't there.

He wouldn't let his disappointment get the better of him. Or that fact that his solitude was over.

Chapter Six

"Where is he?" Will shouted over the noise of the crowd.

Since they'd arrived and done their sound check, Josie noticed that scores of people had since crowded into the fairgrounds for the afternoon concert.

"Who are you looking for?"

Leaning over the soundboard, Will barked at her, his frown darkening his expression. "The kid. He's got an interview with some local news station in ten minutes and I can't find him."

"They're going on stage in fifteen."

"Like I don't know that," he drawled. "I set up the interview for when he's ready to go on stage."

"He's not with the rest of the band?"

Will shook his head. "One guy is ready to do a write-up on Brock and get it to press tonight. We need the press to ensure tomorrow's performance is packed."

Josie searched her mind. The last time she'd seen

Brock he was heading into the crowd around the same time she'd come out to recheck the equipment. She always wanted to make sure the board was undisturbed. When the band went on stage, she didn't want to discover someone had pulled a connection accidentally.

"I haven't seen him since I came out here. Are you sure he isn't with the rest of the band?"

"No, they're all backstage—except for Brock." She glanced out into the sea of people, to the place where she'd last seen Brock. Today he could walk among the crowd and only be noticed for being the handsome man he was. Tomorrow, his picture might be splashed across the pages of the newspaper.

"Where would he go?" Will's face was almost accusing and it gnawed at Josie to think he somehow blamed her for Brock's absence now. "Come on, Josie. The kid's been tight with you," Will continued impatiently when she didn't answer.

It had been true to some degree. But Brock hadn't asked her to stay behind and wait for him to get through with his interviews. Even though she'd been tempted to do just that, she decided the time away, not only from the bus but from the band would be good. But instead of frittering away the afternoon like a tourist alone, she'd spent her down time at the local Laundromat dizzily watching her clothes dry.

Boring, yes. But she'd spent the entire time thinking about Brock and wishing she'd stayed on the bus, if only to have a few minutes alone with him. She enjoyed his company, and she loved his outlook on life as well as his determination to succeed in his dreams.

Will always called Brock "the kid," but Josie knew

there was a wisdom about Brock that made him much older than his years. She could see it in his eyes, hear it in the things he said. No matter how much she tried to remain focused on her goals, there was a part of her that sought out Brock, the man, despite her knowing she shouldn't.

"You keep the news crew happy," she said, grabbing her bottle of water from where it rested on the console. "I'll see if I can find him."

Josie dodged people as she made her way to the one place she thought Brock might escape to. But when she swung open the door to the bus, she found he wasn't there.

She moved down the center aisle of the bus to see if he was in his bunk. It was empty and his guitar was gone.

Earlier, Brock had gone out into the crowd with his guitar in hand. Will's reference to the two of them being "tight" held some truth. They'd certainly gotten much closer. However, their romantic relationship had come to a dead halt since that first day they'd kissed.

Perhaps Brock had become fed up with trying to move their relationship forward and had moved on to one of the many girls who always seemed to be working her way backstage or hanging around the bus before a performance. It wasn't like a girl would be hard to find. They were all beautiful and willing to hook up with a musician.

Josie closed her eyes as jealousy made its way through her veins.

Disgusted with herself for being upset, Josie swung around and walked past her unmade bunk. Dexter's empty kennel lay on top of the bare mattress next to the laundry she'd recently folded and put in her pillowcase. When she'd returned to the bus, she hadn't had time to make her bed. Now it looked baron, especially without her beloved cat stretched out on it.

"Dex?"

Turning toward the kitchen, she found an empty bowl on the counter. Dexter was sitting next to it, licking his paws as if he'd savored whatever had been left in the bowl.

"Dexter, no." She pulled the cat from the counter and brought him to the kennel, stroking his fur as she went. She dropped the cat on the bunk and opened the kennel door. Guilt ate at her as she coaxed Dex inside. She normally let him wander when no one was on the bus, but he'd already gotten into too many things and the end of the tour was still at least two weeks away. Two more weeks before they'd reach Nashville and she could set her plans into action.

"You have to behave, Dexter," she said, looking through the cage's door as her cat meowed, his wide eyes pleading for freedom. "I don't want to have to keep you kenneled all the time. I'll be back in a few hours. I promise to give you my undivided attention then."

At least Dex was the one thing she loved that would never let her down.

"Brock, I came all the way from Houston!"

"Brock, this way. My name is Louise."

"Just a little hug, Brock. Can I have my picture taken with you?"

"We love you Brock!"

They all shouted and grabbed and pulled at Brock as he made his way from the stage toward the tent that was their makeshift dressing room. While he had to admit the fans' excitement was contagious and added to the rise he felt while on stage, he couldn't wait to get back on the bus.

We love you Brock.

He could see it in their eyes. They'd had fun. From on stage he could see them dancing in the crowd, clapping wildly and stomping their feet to the music. They'd remember his name. But they'd never know him. That was never more evident to him than after the string of reporters asking him the same trite questions that could apply to just about any country singer in the industry.

He slipped into the tent and blinked as his eyes adjusted to the change of light. There was a long buffet table with food sitting in trays of ice to keep it from spoiling in the heat. The rest of the band was already there, popping the tops off cans of soda or sipping from bottles of water.

Josie unscrewed a bottle of Evian and took a long drink, wiping her sweat-drenched forehead with the back of her hand. Pink tinged her cheeks and the tip of her nose from being out in the brutal sun for too long.

Brock made his way toward Josie, but stopped when Will stepped in front of him.

"They were eating you up, kid," Will said, slapping Brock on the back. "Get a drink, refresh yourself, and catch your breath. Then come on outside for a meet and greet with the fans and reporters. Did you hear them chanting your name? It was great."

Will handed him an open beer and Brock took a long drink from the can.

"I need a minute to take a breather," he said, releasing his breath.

"Sure, sure. You take whatever you need. But only a second though. We're on a roll. I don't want those reporters leaving before we get a chance to get some pictures with the fans. I'll get the crowd together, set the stage, and let them know you're going to come out to see them."

Brock groaned inwardly. *More reporters.* Josie looked at him, tilting a questioning eyebrow. She was holding her sweating bottle of water to her lips and not drinking. She pulled the bottle away from her mouth and set it on a nearby table.

Josie chuckled and shook her head. "Do you suppose he came out of the womb that way?"

He liked the way she teased and eased his mind.

Her smile faded as she studied him. "You don't like the reporters very much. That much is obvious."

His discomfort wasn't lost to her. It never was.

"What I don't like is feeling like a puppet."

She shrugged and brushed her hand on his shoulder. "Unfortunately, it comes with the territory. They've got the power to spread the word about your music. Like it or not, you need them."

Brock understood that, even if he didn't like having to play the game. "The crowd is great. I love meeting the fans and seeing how excited they are about my music."

Josie picked up her bottled water from the table, opened it, and took a sip. She looked up at him again, seeing into his soul in a way no other woman had ever done.

"You did great out there."

"Thanks."

"Then what's the gloomy face all about?"

Steeling a glance at the tent door for Will, he shrugged. In a minute, Will would be back, waving at him to go back out into that chaos.

"Nothing ever gets past you, does it? I guess I'm just a little tired," he lied.

She stared at him for a lingering moment. "Overwhelmed? You're entitled. The energy on that stage was incredible. It's like that every night. No wonder you sleep like a baby on the bus."

"Thanks for being here," he said, reaching out and brushing a strand of hair away from her face.

"My pleasure." Standing on her toes, she kissed his lips softly. He was just about to drag her into his arms for the kind of embrace he'd been dreaming about all week when Will appeared at the door of the tent and motioned to Brock to come out to meet the fans.

He groaned. "I guess I'm on again."

"I swear he times it that way." The disappointment in her eyes mirrored how Brock felt. "Well, cowboy, go give 'em what they want," she said, brushing her hand across his back.

"Not before I do this," he said. Bending his head, he pressed his mouth to hers, drinking in what he was thirsty for—the sweet tenderness of Josie. And when he pulled away, she was smiling up at him, making his heart sing.

He'd smile for the crowd and give them what they wanted. But what Brock wanted more than anything right at that moment was to just stay under that tent and watch Josie's smiling face. Instead, he handed her his beer and headed for the tent door.

The warm, familiar lump at Josie's feet was a comforting reminded she wasn't alone in the world. She heard the steady breathing and occasional quiet sigh and knew Dexter was sound asleep. Unfortunately, even after the long day she'd spent in the sun, sleep eluded her.

Pulling back the small curtain that covered the window in her bunk, Josie noticed a big, bright, yellow moon hanging high above the earth, dropping moonbeams down from the sky. The cloudless day made it impossible not to notice the beauty of the night.

The bus was still parked at the beach where they did the show. A few of the band members had wanted to get motel rooms and sleep in decent beds, but Will said they'd save that for when they reached Nashville.

Now that the crowd was gone, there wasn't a sound outside but the rumble of the surf. It should have helped lull her to sleep, but instead, she tossed in her bed, upsetting Dexter every time she moved.

As small as her bed was, she'd gotten used to sleeping on the bus as it rolled along the highway. Maybe that's why she was having such a hard time sleeping tonight. She'd totally disrupted her normal schedule, not that there'd been much of one since she'd left home. While each town brought something new on this adventure, there was still a repetition of mundane tasks and a schedule that was impossible to set your watch by. There was often a rush to set up, break down, and stay on schedule only to be holed up later in the bus with nothing to do for hours on end.

Before she'd left home, she'd remembered how tiring it could be on the road and how boredom could overwhelm you if you didn't plan to have something to take your mind off the idleness. Preparing for that, Josie had remembered to toss a few books she'd been meaning to read into her bag along with some knitting she'd started far too many years ago and never seemed to finish. She hadn't yet pulled out the yarn, but the books had been a good addition to her duffle.

It was easier to fill the days than to get through the nights, she found. In the quiet of the night, she often found herself thinking back to past mistakes and regrets. Leaving home so young hadn't seemed like a bad idea at the time, but she'd paid the price of her impulsiveness over the years. She couldn't change the past or take back the pain she'd caused her family any more than Grant Davies could ease the hurt she'd felt after his betrayal.

But that was in her past. This road trip was meant to right the wrongs she could change. No regrets. Brock Gentry had pulled her out of a spiraling path to nowhere and helped her get back on track. For that she'd always be grateful.

She yawned, and even though she couldn't sleep, fatigue pulled at her. At night she could admit to herself the things she refused to acknowledge during the day, during the moments when Brock's warm blue eyes would smile at her from the other side of the bus or when he was on stage and seemed to look out into the crowd and sing only to her. There were moments when she felt as though they were the only two people on earth. Just her and Brock.

It was a nice fantasy that she'd allowed herself every so often. There was so much more to what she felt for Brock than just gratitude. It was those feelings that she feared the most, the ones that made her forget the plans she'd mapped out on paper that day when she'd wrestled with whether or not to go on this road trip. The last thing she wanted was to repeat a history that had ended with her heart being ripped to shreds.

She flung the curtain closed, shutting out the bright moon. She rolled over to her side, punching her pillow twice for good measure. Dexter gave her only a mild protest for disturbing his peace again and quickly settled. She envied her small friend. If only she could do the same.

"Josie? Are you awake?"

Josie's heart leaped to her throat with the sound of Brock's whispered voice.

Pulling back the privacy curtain, she looked up at him in the darkness. "What are you doing up?"

"Same as you. Can't sleep."

Her heart lifted a notch, glad for the company. "I would have thought you'd be dead tired after today."

Brock crouched down to where she was and leaned forward. Though she'd pulled the curtain closed in order to keep the moonlight from shining in, she now regretted it. There was minimal light in the aisle and she could barely make out the contours of Brock's face. But she imagined him smiling down at her, his dimple marking his cheek, teasing her.

From the back of the bus, the sounds of deep breathing and the occasional snort and snore broke the silence.

"Let's get out of here," he said, a mischievous tone in his voice.

Chapter Seven

"**R**ight now? It's the middle of the night, Brock."

"Do you know of a better time when we won't be hounded by people?"

"No." Excitement replaced the fatigue she'd felt earlier.

"There are no fans around. No reporters to meet with. Best of all, Will is asleep and can't promise me to anyone."

"Ooh, sounds fabulous."

"It's just you and me. We've got the beach all to ourselves. I'm already dressed. I'll give you a few minutes and meet you outside the bus."

A few minutes later, after she'd pulled on a pair of comfortable jeans and an oversized sweatshirt, Josie climbed down the bus steps and found Brock standing there. His head was tilted up to the clear sky that was illuminated by the moon. In his hands, he held what looked like a bucket.

"In a way it's too bad there is a full moon tonight," he said.

"Why? I think it's beautiful." She wrapped the small blanket she'd taken from her bunk around her shoulders.

"It is, but it's so bright it covers the stars."

She glanced down at the bucket in his hand. "What's this?"

He turned to her and flashed a playful smile. His hair shone bright and golden against the light of the moon.

"You'll see. Come with me."

He transferred the bucket to the other hand and lazily draped his arm around her. She was glad for the blanket, but the heat she felt from Brock was much more inviting.

When they reached the end of the parking lot, he turned to her. Reaching out, he clasped his hand over hers as they descended the steps together.

Despite her every attempt to convince herself it meant nothing, something warm and wonderful brewed in her stomach with his gesture. It was clear he'd been taught his manners well. He was a gentleman who didn't wear a blue suit and work a normal nine to five job. Brock was a man clad in denim, who held a guitar and a captive audience with his songs. And no matter what she did to stop it, in these short weeks, he'd captured her heart as well.

"I'd never seen the ocean until I left home," she said. It was the first tour with Grant, something similar to the gig they'd done at the festival. She and Grant hadn't spent a moonlit night on the beach and for that she was grateful. Josie wanted to enjoy this precious time alone with Brock without old memories intruding, then leaving her cold as they always did. She didn't want to think about the band or where they were going. She just wanted to enjoy Brock.

"We went once, as kids. An old-fashioned family vacation." He sputtered as if remembering an old joke but was keeping it to himself. But then he said, "My parents loaded all four of us into the minivan and headed to the coast. I remember my mother was at her wits end with all of us, mostly my older brothers, who were at that age when a brawl at the dinner table was a daily event. I think Cody and Beau fought the entire way. Jackson just sat back, like he always did, and kept score of who was winning."

He laughed, but Josie could tell the memory was bittersweet.

"I don't know what made mom think she was going to get a break from all the chaos in the house."

Sand was seeping into her sneakers, making her feet uncomfortable. Josie slipped off her shoes and pulled at her socks, tucking them securely inside the shoes and hooked the combo on her fingers. The smooth sand chilled her feet, but was welcome.

"This looks like a pretty good spot," Brock said, dropping the bucket and crouching down to look at the surf tumbling in to shore.

"For what?"

"Building a sandcastle." He glanced up at her with a playful smile.

Her hands flew to her cheeks. "Are you out of your mind? A sandcastle?"

"Yeah, I've never done this before. Have you?"

"No."

"Then I guess it's a good thing no one is around to watch us do this or it could be really embarrassing."

Josie laughed and let the blanket slip off her shoulders. She dropped it on a dry area of sand a few yards from where they were working and plopped her sneakers on top.

"Even though the gulf water is warm, your feet are going to get cold," he warned.

"You've got to live dangerously once in a while," she teased, watching him dig what looked like a trench about twenty feet in diameter a few yards from the water's edge.

She propped her hands on her hips. "Do you have a blueprint for this sandcastle? That looks awfully big."

"Does it? I'm just winging it."

She laughed. "You didn't say we were building the Coliseum."

"Ah, I could use a little help here," he teased, leaning back on his heels in a crouched position.

"What do you want me to do?"

"Fill the bucket with wet sand. I guess we'll start packing a foundation around the inside of the trench and figure out the rest as we go along."

They worked for an hour or so, piling sand and smoothing the edges until the wall of the fortress was formed.

She'd been thinking about Brock all night, wanting time with him alone. She'd wondered about today—where he'd been and, more importantly, who he'd been with—when Will couldn't find him before the performance.

"Did you enjoy the afternoon?" she finally asked.

He flashed her a smile. "I missed you. I came back to the bus and you weren't there."

"I was going to wait for you, but . . ."

"You don't have to wait around for me, Josie. I don't want you missing the sites just because Will's got me tied up."

Rolling her eyes she said, "Fine sites I saw today. I did laundry."

"Don't let the boys get wind of it. They'll hit you up to do theirs."

"They already did, but I told them they were on their own."

He laughed and dumped a pile of sand in the center. A warm gust of gulf breeze blew his hair all around. He was so handsome, she had to pull her gaze away.

"You showed up just in the nick of time before the show today. I thought Will was going to have a coronary."

Brock packed the sand down with his hand while she waited for him to answer. "The crowd was pretty thick by the time I headed out to the stage. It took longer than I expected."

"Did you catch that reporter he was so anxious for you to meet with before the show?"

Brock looked at his work and seemed satisfied, then stood. "Yeah, I met him." He strode back out toward the tide and filled the bucket with more wet sand.

Josie's heart pumped, unable to voice the questions she so desperately wanted answered.

She didn't say anything when he returned, just stared at him.

"He called me a clown," Brock said, shaking his

head. The hurt in his voice was heart wrenching. It wasn't at all what she'd expected.

"A clown. What for?"

"It's the darned clothes. I feel like a Vegas lounge singer."

Josie shook her head and chuckled softly, mostly to rid herself of the tension plaguing her.

"Brock, he wasn't calling *you* a clown, just the clothes. And from what I understand, this reporter is notorious for ripping performers apart. He has a wide readership but everyone knows he goes for sensationalism in his column. You shouldn't let it bother you. Regardless of what he said, the publicity is good."

"He called me a clown, Josie." Brock wiped the sand from his hands as if he were trying to get rid of his disgust over the whole thing. "He wasn't interested in anything about my music at all. Nothing about me or what we were working for."

"My point exactly." She softened her voice. "Look, you have to put this into perspective. He was making a comment about your clothes. So what? He wasn't calling Brock Gentry, the man, a clown."

"He might as well have. And now all those fans who were enjoying themselves today are going to read that crap and—"

"What, change their minds? I don't think so. If that was the case, Grant Davies would still be flipping burgers at the Radio Grill."

Brock shot a quick glance up at her with the mention of Grant and Josie immediately regretted using him as an example. It had been a natural instinct. She shared a history of the beginning of Grant Davies' career. She couldn't pretend it had never happened, nor did she really want to despite the hurt it caused.

She'd already made the blunder. She decided she might as well go the distance. Years ago, she never would have been brave enough to voice her thoughts or distress to Grant. She wouldn't make that mistake again with Brock. "Where did you go today?" she asked, biting her lower lip.

"I needed some space, so I took a walk. I just wanted to be alone to clear my head about a few things. I found this quiet spot at the end of the beach and sat by myself for a while." His eyes never left hers and she had a feeling he knew what she was asking. "If I was going to be with anyone, Josie, I'd be with you."

Her heart skipped a beat and she felt relief wash over her. *He'd been alone.*

They continued their work on the sandcastle. Inside the twenty-foot wall of sand, they built a small castle that looked out over the ocean. The tide was rolling in and had reached the edge of the trench when they finally finished.

"No one is ever going to see this. It'll be washed away before the sun even comes up," Josie said, her heart tugging with the idea that all their work would soon be lost to the ocean.

"It's okay. It's a Kodak moment." He pulled a small camera from his pocket. With the flash of a grin, he looked into the lens and snapped the picture of her.

She laughed. "Is that a digital camera?"

"Sure is."

"Do you think Will would mind letting you use his laptop for us to show the guys?"

He snapped a few pictures of the sandcastle, then moved to the back of it and, facing the water, caught a great shot of the moon sinking over the top of the castle in the horizon.

Snapping another picture of her, he said, "This is our little secret. We don't have to share it with anyone."

Her belly burned with memories. "You mean you want to be discrete," she said, her voice low. She closed her eyes and called herself every kind of fool.

"Not at all. I don't care if the world knows how I feel about you, Josie. In fact, I wouldn't mind at all if I could scream it out from stage if I knew it wouldn't embarrass you. It's just that some things I don't want to share. Like tonight. Does that make sense?"

Relief replaced her bitter feelings. "Yes, it does."

"There's got to be some place around here we can drop the disk for processing and have it catch up to us later on," he said, looking through the viewfinder to see his work.

"Do you know what hotel we're staying at in Nashville?"

"Will has it on the agenda. Good idea. We'll snap a few pictures and drop the film off on our way out of Galveston. The hotel will hold them for us until we get there."

The night they'd shared—and the pictures—belonged only to them. Josie liked knowing not every waking moment needed to be about the band or shared with them. She couldn't image a more perfect night she'd spent with anyone.

In an hour or so, not only would their new castle be

gone, but the sun would be high in the sky and their time alone would end.

The sea sprayed up little droplets of salt water as they walked barefoot along the wet sand in silence. Brock took Josie's hand again, leading without really insisting they take any particular direction. The beach was much different at night than it had been during the day when it was crowded with people bumping into each other and kicking up sand. Now, as the moon slid behind the occasional cloud and then popped back again, it was peaceful, intimate in a way Josie had missed since they'd set out on the road. It was easy to be with Brock, enjoying the silence, the company, and not demanding anything more from each other.

They walked as far as a hot dog stand that had been boarded up for the night. The smell of fried food still permeated the air around the tiny shack and mingled with the smell of the gulf.

As they made their way back up the beach toward the sandcastle, Josie spotted a park bench by the parking lot that gave them a perfect view of their work. "Want to sit for a bit?"

With a protective hand on the small of her back, Brock led her to the bench. He arranged the blanket over her shoulders and settled back next to her. Even with the shield of the blanket, his warmth radiated all around her. Although there was a heavier breeze whipping in from the Gulf of Mexico, she wasn't bothered by the slight chill that hit her face or bare toes.

"Things were a little crazy today," he said quietly.

The moon had come out of hiding again. Josie could

see Brock's profile clearly. Strong, sure, but his expression was anything but. Troubled lines marred his normally playful expression.

"It gets like that sometimes."

Leaning his arm across the bench behind her, he pulled her closer. "The show was great, though, despite what the critics said."

"You can't let a few music critics get you down. Not everyone is going to see your music like you do. What matters is that crowd. They loved you."

He didn't look convinced and kept staring out at the sea.

"What's eating you?"

With a quick flash of a smile, he glanced at her. "Not a thing. This makes me happy, being here with you like this."

She chuckled softly. "I don't believe you."

"You don't think I enjoy spending time with you?"

"I think you're covering up what's really bothering you."

"That's because you see me as I am. I mean, really see me, not just what you want me to be. And that's the difference that matters."

She looked up at him and waited.

Brock gave an idle shrug. "I don't know what it is. Each day things get bigger and bigger for us—the band, Will, and everything he's doing. Sometimes my head just spins."

He sighed, picking up a handful of sand and letting it sift through his fingers.

"There are people expecting things from me. It's overwhelming to think it's not just about playing my music anymore. There are reporters, promoters, and Will."

She raised her eyebrows. "And Will." Will alone was overwhelming at times, but they both knew he was good at what he did.

"I keep thinking something is missing. Sometimes when I'm playing, I think I've found it. Things seem right on stage. But then it seems to vanish again with the flashbulbs and people pulling at me. I begin to wonder how I lost myself in all this."

The lopsided grin he flashed her made her heart thump. "I guess I didn't expect so many people wanting something more than just my music."

"Yeah, right! Those women asking you to sign their T-shirts this afternoon only came for the music," she drawled.

He laughed. "Yeah, I guess you're right. But that's not what I want."

"What do you want?" She stared at him for what seemed like a full minute while he thought.

Brock shrugged. "To look at our sand castle."

She chuckled softly. "Be serious."

"I am. Right at this moment, this is exactly what I want. I don't want to be anywhere else or with anyone but with you. Things seem right when I'm with you, less overwhelming."

Something warm and wonderful began to brew deep in her soul. It was easy to believe his words, and she longed for them to be true. But warning bells clanged inside her, bringing up memories from her past she didn't want to revisit.

"I've had people around me all my life," he said.

"Coming from a big family, you can't get away from people. Living on a ranch there are always workers running about. But there's plenty of wide-open space too—like this." He swept his right hand toward the ocean and paused a moment. "It makes you feel small, lets you know there's something out there that's bigger than just you. The world's not going to end if you suddenly went away. I'm not used to all the attention being on me."

"You're not in so deep that you can't walk away from it all."

"That's just it. I don't want to. For as long as I can remember, I've wanted this—to be on the stage and to sing my songs. I love what's happening, where we're going. But I know what you mean about not having a moment's peace. I meet so many people, yet it all seems so impersonal, like no one really knows me at all—or really wants to, for that matter. I'm the main attraction but totally insignificant in any way that matters. It's all so cold."

Josie reached out and touched his cheek with her fingers. Brock leaned into her touch and gazed down at her.

"I wish I could say it'll be different."

"I know. Moments like this when it's just you and me are nice though. I like it this way, like it was in the studio that night."

Josie pulled her hand away and adjusted the blanket so it was covering her shoulders, clutching her hands tight across her chest. There'd been a million stars in the sky winking down at them as they'd built their little sandcastle. More than a few times during the evening she'd looked at the sky and really studied the stars.

Over the city, the lights drowned out a good deal of the night sky, making it impossible to really see. But over the ocean, the stars blazed brightly. Now they were losing numbers, hiding behind clouds that had rolled in.

Their time together tonight had made her feel brave in a way she hadn't felt in a long time. The sensation made it easier to talk and to let go of secrets that always seemed to haunt her during the daylight hours.

Josie bit her bottom lip and drew in a breath of salted air for courage. "You've never asked me about Grant."

Chapter Eight

"**I** figured you'd tell me in your own time. I know the two of you were an item."

She snapped her gaze to him, surprised he knew even that much. The wind blew her hair up in circles around her face, making it hard to see him even in the moonlight.

"Did you get that straight from the person who told you where to find me?"

"It's no big deal. We don't have to talk about it if it upsets you."

"That's where you're wrong. It was very much a big deal. I gave up everything for Grant Davies," she said, bitterness bubbling up in her throat with the words. The pain of his betrayal still stung.

"You were what, seventeen?"

"Just shy of my eighteenth birthday when I met him." She shook her head. It all seemed so long ago and yet it was still fresh in her mind, sharp as the pain of remembering it. "You do stupid things when you're young."

Josie hiked the blanket up around her shoulders and felt the grit of sand that clung to it fall beneath her shirt, making her as uncomfortable as the subject they were discussing.

"Grant was just a local then. No one in Nashville knew him. My friends and I used to sneak out of the house and go down to the fairs to hear music. My girl-friends wanted to meet the musicians, but I was just a sponge hanging around the sound engineers. I was always so fascinated with what they were doing. I used to talk to the techies while my friends were grabbing autographs and pretty soon I began to learn." She paused, revisiting the past, then continued with her story.

"One night we met Grant. It was his first time in the area and his band was still trying to work out all the kinks of playing live. He had an argument with his regular sound man and the guy took off right before the show."

"That sounds vaguely familiar," Brock said, chuckling.

"I'd been talking to the sound man before Grant came by. I was just standing there during the argument, and when it was clear the sound man wasn't coming back by the time the band was due to play, Grant pointed to me and said, 'You're my girl. I need you to do sound for me tonight.' I was scared. I didn't know anything about doing live sound except what I'd learned and then used back at school. They'd already done a sound check. All I had to do was run the board and make sure nothing happened during the performance."

"And nothing did."

She eyed him. "Did you hear this story before or are you going to let me tell it?"

Laughing, he said, "I'm your captive audience."

"It was pure luck things went off without a hitch. It was fun and I felt important for the first time in my life, like I could do something I really loved. Grant asked me to come to the next show and then the next. I was . . . smitten." She knew it had actually been more starry-eyed and more like a lovesick puppy, but it hurt too much to think she'd made mistakes for something so trivial.

"He talked big, saying he was saving up for a road trip and needed to do some demos to shop around and give to radio stations along the way and to record companies. He just didn't have the cash for studio time."

She sighed. "I was eager to help."

"How'd he luck out?"

She knew Brock was referring to the hard time she'd given him about working with him in the studio. "I was naive back then."

"And now you're worldly and wise?"

Her laughter caught on the wind and sounded far away.

"Hardly. Just a little more mature."

"I like that about you."

Josie looked at the sky, feeling the cool breeze caress her cheeks. "I'd been working in the school studio doing some projects, so I offered to lay some tracks for him there. It was the right price—free—and it gave me the opportunity to work on his music." And be with Grant. She didn't have to add that because Brock already knew they had been involved. "There was nothing fancy about the studio, just basic equipment. The sound was pretty primitive by Nashville standards."

"It shows how talented you are. You got Grant noticed by the bigwigs in Nashville. That sound set him apart from the others."

The blush that crept up her cheeks warmed her face. "Thank you. Anyway, our relationship was discrete. His idea. He said no one would take me seriously as a sound engineer if they thought we were dating. I thought I was falling in love when he asked me to go on the road with him."

"At barely eighteen?"

Closing her eyes to the memory, she sighed. "Yep, my mother was livid. I'd just turned eighteen and told her I was going on the road with a country singer. We fought for days and when the morning came for me to leave, she told me if I walked out that door, it would be the last time I ever saw her. She was right."

Brock's arms squeezed her shoulders in comfort. Josie was glad the moon had sailed behind a cloud and kept his face from view. Her bottom lip quivered and she had to push the words past her throat.

"I never went home and she never contacted me. My father called when they put her in a nursing home a few years ago. She has Alzheimer's and doesn't remember me at all now."

"Do you see your dad?"

Hot tears she hadn't shed in a long time slid down her cheeks, making her shiver. She swiped her face hard. "No, he died last year of a heart attack. I went to the funeral. I saw my mother for the first time in years, but she didn't see me. She looked right at my face and didn't know who I was."

"I'm sorry," he said softly.

"Me too. We left a lot of things unsaid because I was stubborn and thought I knew everything there was to know."

"You were young."

Laughing wryly, she said, "I was stupid. I promised myself that day there would be no more regrets."

"Is that why you decided to go back on the road?"

"Yes. It was time."

He smiled. "It took some convincing. Are you sure?"

She shrugged. "I was scared. Back then, I thought I knew what I wanted. Only I didn't see what was really there. It slammed hard into my face one day in Nashville though. You see, I was in love with Grant Davies, a man who was going straight to the top of the charts. He was loving every pretty face that smiled at him, only I was too blind to see it."

Bitterness ate at her words. She remembered the first time she'd found Grant back stage holding another woman in his arms, speaking the same words he'd spoken to her just hours before. She learned that day they were just words he gave away freely. Nothing heartfelt.

Blowing out a quick breath, she shook herself of the pain.

"The guy's an idiot."

With a roll of her eyes, she said, "He's a man. Brock, you can't say that you haven't seen temptation staring at you in the faces of all those women who have been calling after you lately. You wouldn't be human otherwise."

Brock shrugged. "It may be a different pretty face, but it's the same old thing."

"Oh, really?" she said, her voice dripping with sarcasm.

"Grant really soured you on men, didn't he?" Brock said, leaning forward and resting his elbows on his knees. She suddenly felt cold with his absence.

"Not all men."

"Just music men. Is that it? The blue suit variety of men are just fine."

"Do you blame me?"

He turned to her but didn't say a word. Instead, he shook his head, picked up some sand and tossed it away.

"I don't want to make the same mistakes I made before. I don't want to have any more regrets. Is it so wrong of me not to want to share a man with every woman in the world? I'm that selfish, you know. I don't want to share the man I love. I want him all to myself."

"Sharing your man on stage and sharing him in your life are two different things."

"How do you know that?"

"Because I do. I've seen it."

"Where?"

"My oldest brother was a famous bronc rider, Beau Gentry. Have you ever heard of him?"

Josie's interest was piqued. "Yes, I have. Beau Gentry is your brother?"

Brock nodded. "I never thought he'd show his face back home, but he's there. He and Mandy, my sister-in-law, take my niece to rodeos now, but years ago it was just Beau. He used to tell me that even after all the women he'd met, he never stopped loving Mandy. There was only one woman for him."

Envy crept through her veins. "That's beautiful."

"It's real. I don't see how it would be different for you and me. Blue suit or not, I'm just a man who happens to want to make a living on the road and come home to the same woman, no matter how many pretty faces come to my door."

Her eyes widened. She wanted to believe him. Josie wanted to think that Brock would be different. But she'd already seen history repeating itself with the other band members over the last week. Women were everywhere, smiling and offering their time. And all the men had their pick. Brock hadn't taken his pick and part of her wanted to believe she was the reason.

"Brock—"

"No, let me finish. I know you're scared of being hurt again. I can see that. But I don't want to let go of what I've found in you."

"And what's that?"

"A true friend."

She sputtered with exaggerated disgust. "Oh, come on, not an 'f' word," she said, trying to keep her voice light. Trying to keep from feeling all these amazing things Brock made her feel when she was with him. She was glad when he laughed at her slip.

"An 'f' word?"

"You know, friend, flattered, fat. It's the three evil 'f' words every woman hates to hear when she's with a man."

"You don't believe friendship is important in a relationship between a man and a woman?"

"Of course it is."

"I'd just like someone who sees me for what I am and accept me for that. My parents weren't friends," he confided. "They were more like business partners, although my brother, Cody, said there was a time when Mom and Dad truly did love each other. I never saw it though."

"That's too bad. Are they still together?"

"Sadly, no. Mom died when I was fifteen." Brock cleared his throat. "Come walk with me." He reached for her hand and the blanket slid off her shoulders. Brock quickly put it back in place and wrapped his arm around her shoulder to keep it there. She felt good and safe in Brock's arms, especially in the vast ocean of uncertainty that had been plaguing her.

"Let's stay here and watch the sun come up over our little sandcastle," Brock said, wrapping the blanket around both of their shoulders and enveloping her with his warmth.

It was a sweet thing to say and Josie couldn't think of anything more romantic. They hadn't talked about the band, or gigs, or anything that had to do with music. Tonight it had been all about them.

Things had changed. She'd gone from seeing Brock as the talented musician he was and as a means for her to break out of the rut she'd dug herself in, to a man she enjoyed being with—someone she genuinely cared for. A man who made her think of fairy-tale endings she'd sworn long ago didn't exist.

"That sounds great." Leaning closer to him, she asked, "Which way is east? I'm so bad with direction."

"It's a good thing you're not driving the bus then."

She giggled as he leaned in and kissed the tip of her

nose. Sucking in a deep breath, Josie lifted her head, parting her lips. Her instinct kicked in. This wasn't a good idea. She'd told herself that very thing over and over again after the first time they'd kissed.

But she ignored the warning bells that clanged in her head and met him half way until his warm mouth covered hers and lingered.

This kiss was much different than the one they'd shared on the bus. The newness was gone, and the mystery of who they were had been solved tonight over the simple, playful act of building a castle out of sand. A new bond had strengthened between them.

Josie tilted her head back, tasting his lips and drawing him closer to her.

When they parted, he brushed away a strand of hair the wind had blown against her face. "No regrets?" he said softly.

"No regrets."

And she meant it. There wasn't anything about tonight she would change, from building their sandcastle to kissing Brock.

"The moon is gone," Josie said, lifting her head to the sky. Clouds that had been teasing them all evening had now filled the sky. "I don't think we're going to get a chance to see the sun come up this morning."

"There'll be other sunrises. I promise you that. I want more nights like this with you, Josie. Holding you just like this." Brock sighed. "I don't really want to go back to the bus. I wish I could find a way to hold back the morning."

The sky was changing from black to blue. As disappointed as she was to see the night end, it didn't take away from the new hope that filled her heart. Their relationship was growing and it felt good.

"Do you think anyone is up?"

"Probably not, but I'd guess that if anyone is, it's Will. In about an hour, Miles and Roy will probably be arguing again."

She quirked a smile. "Forget the sunrise. I'll make us some scrambled eggs. We can sit back and watch Miles and Roy argue. You can be the one to keep score this time."

They walked hand in hand back to the bus. The blanket was filled with sand. They each took a corner and shook it out before folding it and climbing on board. The smell of coffee already filled the bus. As suspected, Will was up, seated at the dining table as he nursed a mug of coffee and poured over paperwork.

"A little early for a walk. Where have the two of you been?" he grumbled sleepily.

Brock glanced over at Josie and gave her a sleepy smile and her heart exploded with emotion. One night of playful fun had given her an enormous view into what this man was all about. As frightened as she was of another broken heart, she couldn't just walk away. She'd give it a chance and let fate play out—with no regrets.

The band had played a long set at a local hot spot in Memphis the night before after spending the day walking around Graceland. Memphis was a music town with an excitement and a charge all its own.

The big test for them would be Nashville.

In each town they played, the crowd was bigger than

the last, the press more interested in Brock Gentry. Josie knew there'd come a day when simply walking down Main Street would be a major event. But for right now, she was enjoying the fact that Brock Gentry was hers and hers alone.

They'd only been scheduled for the one show in Memphis and were due to leave this morning for a four-hour drive out to Nashville. Brock said he couldn't leave Memphis without at least seeing a little of the city, so they snuck out of the bus just as the sun was rising and walked the streets, hand in hand, until they found an open door.

"Let's get out of here before Will promises my time to some reporter," he'd said, and just as the sun rose they'd both run from the bus like two kids sneaking out of the house for some fun.

They found a small, hole-in-the-wall diner in downtown Memphis that was filled with the smell of fresh coffee and baked bread. She pulled Brock through the door and sat in the quiet of the morning before the rest of the world started milling around the streets, going about their days.

As the waitress dropped the Sunday breakfast special of fried grits, eggs over easy, and buttered whole wheat toast in front of Brock, Josie nursed her coffee and played with her napkin. She'd only ordered a bagel with cream cheese, but didn't feel like eating.

"Not hungry?" Brock asked, motioning to her untouched plate.

"It's too early for me to eat. I'll wrap it up and take it back to the bus."

"You'd better hide it from Roy."

She chuckled at his teasing.

Most of their meals were spent with the band, which was fine by Josie on most days. But in the time since they'd spent that precious night building their sandcastle together, Brock had taken her seriously when she said she didn't want their relationship to only be centered around the band. He made a noticeable effort to pull her away so they could share time alone.

"It almost doesn't seem real that the next stop is Nashville," she said, ringing her napkin and then tossing it to the table with a sigh.

He swallowed his food and took a sip of coffee. "I think I'm looking forward to sleeping in a real bed instead of in that small bunk."

"Yeah, I guess you boys have it rougher than I do. I don't think I could stand one more night of Roy and Miles going at it."

"It hasn't been all that bad, has it?"

She shook her head. "When I decided to come, I figured I knew pretty much how things would go. I didn't count on you though."

Brock lifted an eyebrow. "Didn't you?"

"Well, you haven't exactly kept your feelings from me. But right from the start you treated me as a professional. It's a hard road for a woman surrounded by men."

"You deserve your place in this just like the rest of us."

"Thanks. Brock, what are you hoping will happen when we get to Nashville?"

He looked surprised by the question. "I'm hoping to catch the eye of one of those A&R reps Will's been talking to for the last few weeks." He reached his hand across the table to squeeze hers. "I'm also hoping to catch my breath a little so we can spend more time together. Isn't that what you want?"

She smiled, her chest filling with emotion. "Absolutely."

"What's troubling you then?"

Josie chuckled as she rolled her eyes. "Nothing really. I guess I'm just a little fearful. I don't want to screw up this time."

In those stolen moments together, their relationship flourished, and Josie found it easy to confess her secrets when she was with Brock. He had a way of digging into her soul with just a smile, unearthing a part of Josie she hadn't known existed. It was hard to put all that into perspective when the end result would mean they could be going their separate ways in Nashville.

"Things could change, you know," she said, looking him straight in the eye.

"Nothing's going to change." He flashed her one of those Brock Gentry look-at-me smiles and she almost believed him.

Of course, he was right. It didn't have to be that way. In the quiet hours alone, Josie could dream about the two of them, building a life and sharing their dreams—together.

It was dangerous, she knew. So many uncertainties lay ahead of them in Nashville. The studio executives became the new dogs of their world and their lives could change in an instant.

Josie refused to let that possibility mar what little time they had now. If all they had was this moment, then she was determined to take it and enjoy it for what it gave her.

As they finished breakfast and left the diner, the quiet peace that surrounded her at the diner remained. No thoughts of an uncertain future intruded on them as they walked the streets of Memphis, hand in hand.

"That is so you," Josie said, laughing as she peered into a storefront window. The black suede cowboy hat sat perched on a stand under white lights to show off its beauty.

"You think so?"

"Definitely. Let's go take a look," she said, pulling him into the store.

The Cowboy Strong was only one of many specialty stores that had just opened, their doors for the day. The salesman greeted them and Josie pulled Brock over to the window where she'd seen the black suede cowboy hat.

Brock raised an eyebrow in jest. "No blue sequins?"

"Thank you, God," she said laughing. Carefully, she lifted the hat from the stand and placed it on Brock's head. The smell of the suede filled her senses and it felt smooth and lush on her fingers. She could imagine how fabulous Brock would look up on stage wearing it. When he stood up straight and looked at her, she realized she was wrong. Her imagination did no justice to how commanding a man Brock looked wearing the hat. Or maybe it was simply the man himself, Josie thought.

"What do you think?"

He actually looked shy as he waited for her approval, cocking his head to one side.

"I don't know how you've lived your whole life without that hat," she teased.

He laughed. "Well, that settles it. I can't put it back on the rack after you put it that way."

"Let me buy it."

His brow creased.

"Come on," she said. "My gift to you." It seemed so small a gift when she compared it to how Brock had changed her world so completely in the short time since he'd walked into the studio back in Houston.

Her heart bursting, she moved to the counter to make the purchase and caught the time on the iron clock on the wall.

"What time did Will say the bus was leaving?" she asked.

"Five minutes ago."

"Oops, guess they left without us." If it weren't for the fact that Dexter was stuck on the bus, Josie would revel in the idea of having that bus roll down the highway without them.

Pulling her into his arms, Brock bent his head and pressed his warm mouth against her lips in a kiss that left her dizzy.

"Thank you," he said.

"You're very welcome, cowboy."

Brock sighed and reached for her hand, squeezing it. "We'd better get back."

"You're late," Will said, glaring at them as they boarded the bus. The air conditioning was on, and it immediately bathed Josie's face with cool air as she made her way down to an empty seat. Brock picked up his guitar and dropped down on the seat next to her, giving her a quick kiss on the cheek.

"We went shopping," he said, seemingly unfettered by Will's disposition.

"Nice hat. We can roll," Will called out to the bus driver before lowering his head to concentrate on his paperwork.

"Me and my back can't wait to get to Nashville and check into that hotel," Miles said.

"I can't say I'm not glad to be sleeping in a real bed again, even if I still have to bunk with the likes of you."

"Just four more hours, boys. The hotel has all the luxuries—Jacuzzi, heated pool, mini bar, you name it. It even has those thick, terry cloth bathrobes and a towel warmer."

Brock smiled and put down the guitar. "I hope there's a jacuzzi for two," he said, pulling Josie into his lap. She laughed as he waggled his eyebrows at her.

"Sure does. It's even big enough for you, Miles," Will said with a laugh. "I want you all rested for the shows at the Wild Horse Saloon. It's going to be a big string of nights, with lots of big names there."

Josie was sitting next to Brock and he gave her a squeeze. "It's pet-friendly, Will, isn't it?" Josie asked.

Will didn't look up from his paperwork at her inquiry. She had the feeling his expression would be a bit frosty if he had. Ever since that night on the beach in Galveston, she and Brock had grown closer. It was nice not to have to hide their feelings like she had when she'd been dating Grant years ago. Brock proved to be openly affectionate, pulling her to his lap and giving her a hug and kiss no matter who was around to witness it.

At first, she'd felt a little self-conscious. But the feelings Brock evoked in her quickly lessened any fears she had. She loved the unabashed affection he had for her and the fact that he didn't seem to mind that anyone might witness it.

"Don't worry," Will said. "The hotel has room for your cat."

She smiled, anticipation racing through her. They'd all been waiting for this day to come. Glancing at Brock, her heart tumbled. Many new beginnings awaited them in Nashville. She only hoped it didn't mean an end to what she'd found with Brock.

Chapter Nine

Whatever anxiety Josie had left over what lay ahead for her and Brock in Nashville changed to excitement the moment the bus pulled into the hotel parking lot.

"You only have about two hours to settle in before we head out for sound check. Oh, and by the way," Will said with a Cheshire cat grin. "We're riding in style too. The limo will be waiting out front at five o'clock sharp."

They all stumbled from the bus, duffle bags in hand. Josie put her duffle down under the large hotel awning and arched her back to get the kinks out.

"That comfortable bed isn't coming too soon," Brock said, picking her bag up and holding it in the same hand he gripped his guitar case.

"I can take it," Josie said.

"It's okay," he said, smiling. "You've got precious cargo."

Josie couldn't help but chuckle at his teasing her

about Dexter. Where Will liked to jab her, Brock had actually gotten used to Dexter. In fact, Dexter was even warming up to Brock.

They all rode the elevator up to the top floor in silence. Josie leaned her head against the wall and closed her eyes.

"I could use a nap, too," Brock said, breaking into the silence just as the elevator door swooshed open.

They reached her door first. After inserting the card key and waiting for the green light, she pushed the door open. The smell of lavender filled her nose. The room was cool and everything smelled fresh and crisp like a spring day.

"This is heavenly," she said, carefully placing Dexter's kennel on the soft floral bedspread. There was only one queen-sized bed, but it looked enormous after sleeping in a small bunk for the last month. By the window was a small table with two cushioned chairs and next to that sat a sofa in perfect position for viewing the television.

Josie fluffed a pillow on the sofa. "Wow. This place is nicer than my apartment back in Texas."

"Yeah, Will really outdid himself." Brock peeked inside the bathroom and made a mocking grimace. "Bummer. It's a whirlpool bath, but it's only big enough for one. I'll have to speak to him about that."

Josie shot Brock a wry grin. "Don't get cute."

"But I am cute. You even think so," he said, waggling his brows.

She laughed as she dropped onto the sofa. Reaching over to the bed, she opened the kennel door, but waited for Dexter to feel comfortable enough to emerge into his new surroundings.

The hotel door closed. She lifted her head in time to see Brock pull the chain to lock it.

"Aren't you going to check out your room?"

"I need a nap," he said in a deep voice as he dropped down to the sofa next to her. With his hands, he gently coaxed her back against his chest as he leaned back on the pillows. "Now this is heaven."

"What are you doing?" Her slight protest was feeble, even to her own ears. Her body melted against Brock's and she felt all the tension in her muscles ease.

"Lady, I've been dying to get you in my arms like this all day," he whispered against her forehead, giving her a warm kiss that made her head spin.

His hands stroked her hair, teasing her. As he spoke softly, she felt his warm breath against her skin.

Placing her hand against the wall of his chest, she allowed herself to relax. "Hmm. I like that thought."

"I've been dreaming of holding you like this and drifting off to sleep for as long as I can remember. Now that I have the chance to do it without any eyes on us, I'm not going to pass it by."

"That's a nice dream," she murmured, her eyes filling with tears. It had been hers too. But in her dreams, the words he spoke were that of his love for her. She'd said the words back a hundred times herself. *Only in her dreams.*

"We should set the alarm or we'll never make it down to the lobby by five o'clock." Josie started to move toward the clock, but Brock held her back.

"You're not going anywhere. If we don't wake in time, someone will come get us."

With that, she settled against his chest and started to drift off to sleep. She couldn't be sure if it was a dream, but she swore she heard him say, "I love you, Josie."

His guitar was gone.

At first, Brock searched the band's dressing room at the Wild Horse Saloon, assuming he'd forgotten where he'd placed it or that perhaps someone had draped a jacket over the case, hiding it from his view. But that never happened. Brock never forgot where he put his guitar. Backstage, he didn't allow it out of his sight for more than a few minutes.

He'd already pulled all the jackets and clothes from the sofa and chairs in the room three times. His guitar was definitely gone, and panic, as strong and painful as a heart attack, was setting in. Beads of sweat popped up on his forehead as he continued searching to no avail.

"The house is packed, Brock," Will said, charging into the room without knocking and dropping right down to the sofa, not caring that he was sitting on someone's jacket.

But the words Will spoke didn't evoke any calm in Brock. In fact, it only made matters worse.

"Do you have any idea who's out there tonight? Huh?" Will raised his eyebrows, his eyes bright and gleaming with excitement. Brock already knew how to read Will. His expression was that of a man who'd just hit the jackpot in Vegas and was ready to horde his stash. Will didn't get this charged over little things. This was big.

"Who?"

"Rick Beckley. He does A&R for Sentry Records. He loved that demo I sent and heard about the trail we've been blazing to Nashville. *He* called *us*. Can you believe it? He called me to tell me he'd be here tonight."

"That's great." Brock said the words but didn't feel any of the excitement. His eyes crawled around the room, searching again, already knowing he wouldn't find what he was looking for, but unable to stop himself.

"I think he would have signed you right on the spot, but he wants to see how you perform live. Most artists make the bulk of their living from live performances and those live shows move record sales. You give the performance of your life tonight, kid, and you've got the gold."

Brock forced a smile. The air in the room was like a vacuum, sucking the fresh air out of his lungs. Will kept talking, but all Brock could think about was his guitar. Someone had taken his guitar.

He could have sworn he'd taken it into the dressing room with him. Of course he did. He always did.

"Come on, kid, what's eating you?" Will slapped him on the back as if Brock were a champion boxer about to go out into the ring. Brock didn't feel like the champion. Instead, it was as if someone had punched his lights out and the world around him was counting to ten as he struggled to pull himself up.

"I told you I'd make you a star and tonight is your night to shine."

The walls of his chest constricted, his muscles squeezing tighter. He had to force his mind to think about his breathing. Just breathe, he told himself. He knew the feeling because he had been plagued with it before. He'd felt it the first night he'd performed in Houston, the night he'd met Will. Somehow he'd managed to move past it enough to get himself on stage that night. He'd done it before. He could do again. He'd be okay if he could make it that far.

His eyes sought out the door. *Breathe steady, clear your mind*, he told himself.

"They're waiting for you, kid. Tonight, it's all going to be yours," Will said, oblivious to Brock's distress.

"I know. Just give me a few minutes."

Brock was vaguely aware of the door closing. He searched the room and realized Will had left. He glanced at his reflection in the dressing room mirror. Lights twinkled all around the perimeter, blinding him so all he could see was the reflection in the center of the glass, a stranger staring back at him. For the first time in his life, he honestly didn't know who he'd become.

He remembered the words of his mother. At times like this, he always thought back to how she'd encouraged him to be who he was. And in a few short weeks, he'd let Will paint a new picture of him until he'd become completely unrecognizable.

After fastening the top button of his shirt, he smoothed down the royal blue satin, watching the lights reflect off the fabric. His heart pounded ferociously. He wasn't this man he saw in the mirror. He didn't think he'd ever be.

Breathe steady.

Sweat bubbled on his forehead. With the back of a shaky hand, Brock wiped it clean. Someone had taken his guitar.

Breathe, he continued his mantra.

His heart rate quickened as a knock on the door pulled him from his musings.

"Everyone's wondering what's keeping you, Brock," Josie said, stepping into the room.

He wanted to weep as emotion surged through him, threatening to break the surface of his composure. Josie. Thank God, it was Josie. The woman calmed his fears and gladdened his heart like no one else had ever done before in his life. Life made sense with Josie around. His little gypsy. He needed her tonight more than he'd ever needed anything.

"I can't . . . do this," he said, scared to say the words out loud. Closing his eyes, he turned away from Josie's bright smile.

With a few slow strides, she was by his side, smiling at him. "Sure you can."

Her voice was smooth and comforting. God, he loved the sound of it, what it did to him. The gentle hand she placed on his shoulder seemed to anchor the room as it spun.

"You've done this same show here every night for nearly a week now. In the last six weeks the band has become so tight. With the crowd that's out there, it's going to be a fabulous show."

He shook his head and turned to her, taking her by the hand. As he swallowed hard, his heart pounded like the wheels of a freight train racing down a track.

"You don't understand. I can't do this. I really can't."

She'd been as excited as the rest of the band about tonight's performance. But the light in her eyes instantly darkened when she saw his drawn expression. Her smile faded, slowly at first, and then the excitement that had lit her face was gone.

"What is it, Brock? Did something happen?"

He shook his head. "My guitar's gone," he said quietly, sinking lower as he heard himself voice his fears. Shame shook him to the core. If he'd been with anyone else, he'd have rather crawled into a hole than admit his fear. But this was Josie. He held her hand tight, his eyes fixed on hers.

She chuckled softly, cocking her head to one side. "Is that what's bothering you?"

"It's gone, Josie."

"No, it's not. It was on stage. I saw it. One of the crew must have taken it for you. Just relax."

"I can't. I usually sit with my guitar and play before a show." He closed his eyes, the walls of the room closing in on him. He looked past her toward the door. He needed air, needed to get out of there. Humiliation washed over him. He hated that Josie was seeing him this way. Dear God, anything but this.

Her frown was back. "Brock, what's wrong?"

"This is different." He took a quick breath. "This is huge." He peered into her blue eyes as she fixed her gaze on his face.

Settling into the chair next to him, she sighed. "It's just a little stage fright, Brock. You can work through it. It'll go away as soon as you start to play."

He swallowed, keeping his eyes steady on Josie.

Thank God she was here. "I can't be what they want. I don't even know what they want."

Her smooth voice was low when she spoke. "You're thinking too much. Just be who you are. That's all they want, Brock. That's all you can be."

"That wasn't good enough in Galveston. That reporter tore me to shreds." He looked at his reflection in the mirror. He *was* a clown. How could he be any-thing but a clown wearing this getup? Shame leveled him as he closed his eyes. "I can't say I blame him."

Her gaze dropped to his shirt and then back at him again. Her face didn't register any emotion, but he knew what she must be thinking.

With a quick sigh, she said, "Who cares what the critics think, Brock? Did you see that crowd out there? Do you hear them?"

Panic slammed into him, leaving his heart beating wildly in his chest until he thought it would burst. "Yeah, I can hear them."

"Good. Because when you look out at that crowd, there'll be a lot of faces you recognize. Some of those people caught buses from Galveston and Houston and they came all the way here to see you."

He drew in a deep breath and bolted to his feet.

Josie was quick to come to his side, placing a tender hand on his shoulder. "Take it easy. You're going to hyperventilate if you don't slow down."

"I can't," he said, his voice in a whisper.

"You have a choice, you know. You don't have to do this," she said, her delicate brows furrowing with concern.

With her words, relief bowled him over like a tidal

wave. He didn't have to do this. He turned to the door. Running away sounded really good right now. He could walk out that door, away from the stage and away from the panic, and he'd be okay.

But he *did* have to do this. What kind of person just walked away from all these people when they expected to see a show? *His* show. They came to see him. What kind of man would he be to just go back on his word?

Closing his eyes, he sighed. He felt his hand tremble and his throat constrict, choking him. *Breathe.*

"How long have you been having panic attacks?" Josie said, taking his hand.

She knew. Of course she did. How could she not? He was practically wetting his pants in fear.

Brock dragged his hand across his face. "My whole life."

He hated admitting it. He hated that it always made him feel so weak. No amount of muscle could move him when the feeling of panic hit him square in the chest.

His brother Beau could face a wild bronc hell-bent on stomping all over him, but Brock couldn't even walk out on stage.

When he'd been a kid, his brothers had razzed him like only brothers could do. His father had called him a coward for letting panic get the best of him. His mother had blamed his father's heavy hand and tough cowboy ways for breaking Brock's spirit and causing the panic attacks in the first place.

But Brock knew none of that was the cause. There were times he could climb up on stage and be fine. He could face a group of people and feel alive. Other times the walls closed in on him without any warning, offering no rational explanation for what brought on the attack. He couldn't predict when he'd feel the panic; he could only use the tools he'd learned over the years to help get through it.

His solution was playing his guitar. But now his guitar was gone.

Josie stood behind him and eased him into the chair by the dressing mirror. Her hands gently kneaded his tight shoulder muscles. He loved her hands. The way they seemed to glide gently over his shoulders pulled the tension away, and pushed his anxiety off. "What do you do when you feel the panic?"

"I play my music. But I can't get up on that stage and let everyone see me this way."

He buried his face in his hands, rubbing his throbbing temples. He didn't know if he was hiding from his attacks or from Josie's probing gaze.

After a few minutes, he turned his head around to look up at her. God, she was beautiful. Her dark hair fell slightly forward, framing her face as she bent her head and worked his muscles.

"That feels good," he said, concentrating on the magic her fingers were making instead of on all the thoughts racing through his mind.

"I'm glad."

He closed his eyes, letting her energy build inside him. His breathing was getting easier, steadier. "You saw my guitar on stage?"

"Someone must have taken it out without thinking.

Everyone is so excited tonight. I'm sure someone did it just to be helpful."

He nodded his head, wishing the situation was different. Someone took what was his, what he needed. But it hadn't been out of malice.

"I need my guitar right now. That must sound so pathetic for a grown man to say."

She chuckled softly. "No, it doesn't. Don't beat yourself up about this. You think you're the only one in the world who carries around a security blanket of sorts?"

When he didn't answer, she went on.

"Why do you think I insisted Dexter come on this road trip? You have your guitar, and I have my cat. Whether Miles and Roy would agree or not, I think they have each other and without the arguing they'd be lost."

Brock chuckled for the first time since the attack hit.

"I always play by myself before a performance. It calms me down when I get nervous. It helps channel my thoughts."

"I haven't seen you like this at all. How have you been hiding this?"

"I haven't had an attack in a long time. That first day in Galveston I thought the walls were closing in on me when I was on the bus alone. I took a walk right out to the water's edge. No one knew who I was there. No one expected anything out of Brock Gentry and for the most part, they didn't pay me any mind at all. It helped."

"I'd wondered where you went that day."

"I was alone, Josie. Even though there was a flood of people around that beach, I was by myself with my guitar. It always helps. I don't know if I can get on that stage. There's so much riding on tonight. So many people are expecting something of me, and if I don't deliver . . ."

"You had your guitar in Galveston. Have you ever had an attack before a performance and just gone on stage without the guitar?"

Brock thought back to the night he'd met Will. He'd nearly lost his dinner that night alongside the drummer of the other band. The weight of his feet had him thinking he was dragging steel across the stage. But when he finally made it to the center of the stage, had the guitar in his hands and the lights hitting his face, he could hardly see the people beyond the border of the stage and he'd convinced himself they weren't even there.

He'd worked through his panic that night because he hated the feeling of being controlled. He'd wanted to impress Will Harlen. He'd wanted it so badly, he faced his fears and just walked on stage.

"Just once in Houston. Back in Steerage Rock, I knew everyone at the dance hall. It was like a big party every night I played. It felt comfortable. This is different."

His chest tightened just thinking about it and he had to force a deep breath to get air.

"How about we do it differently tonight then? Do it like you did that one night in Houston."

"I was by myself that night. I didn't have the band."

"Okay. You could start on the stage alone instead of with the rest of the band. Do an acoustic number and then the band could join you after you feel comfortable again."

Brock shook his head. "That's just it. I don't think I can do it at all."

Josie continued to rub his shoulders and play with the hair at the nape of his neck. "Sure you can. Just pretend you're back in the studio when you sang that night we were alone. Don't think about what's beyond the lights. Pretend it's just you and me again trying to lay down some tracks. That's all. I'll be right beyond the lights looking back at you, just like I was there beyond the glass in the control room that night. It'll be just you and me, Brock. Don't think about anyone else."

Just him and Josie. He liked the idea of that. It was easy for him to be with her, easy to admit his fears and relax.

"Will doesn't know," he said.

"I don't doubt it. He's too wrapped up in trying to promote you right now. But he's going to know if you don't go on that stage in the next five minutes."

Just him and Josie. He could do that.

Josie stopped her massage and rested her hand on his shoulder, giving him a quick kiss on the top of his head. Their eyes met and locked in their reflections in the mirror. He couldn't imagine going through this without her. Having Josie in his life, in this room right now, made all the difference in the world.

Five minutes ago, his mind was searching for a way to escape. In just a short time, she'd calmed his nerves and steadied his breathing. Although some of the panic remained, it had ebbed considerably and that all-consuming fear was fading.

"Like I said, you don't have to go out there, Brock. No one, not even Will, can make you. But just think for a minute about what you'll be missing. These people are just regular people like you and me who've come to share a moment with you. That's all. Just a moment in time. You can share it with them or you can walk away.

That's your choice. But if you walk away, the moment is lost forever. You can't get it back."

"You sound like you're talking from experience."

Her crooked smile was bittersweet, but her eyes twinkled from the moisture filling them. "I made a promise to myself when I boarded the bus for this trip—no regrets. Do you think you can walk away and not regret this? That's what you have to ask yourself."

Brock stared at the mirror. He didn't see a man he recognized there and that scared him to death.

"Give me a minute. Tell Will I just need a minute."

"Brock?" she started.

He looked directly in her eyes so she would know he was speaking the truth. "I'll be there. I promise."

Josie bent her head and kissed his forehead, then his lips. The sweet kisses magically did wonders to calm his nerves. He wanted more though. He wanted to wrap her in his arms and hold her by his side, and be as close as they'd been earlier at the hotel. He wanted everything that was good and wonderful about this woman to envelope him and wash away the rest of his fears. Having her on the other side of the auditorium was too far.

"No regrets," she whispered as she slipped out of the dressing room. He heard her shoes on the floor as she made her way down the hallway toward the stage.

Brock took a long hard look at himself in the mirror again and quickly unbuttoned the royal blue satin shirt.

The stage was empty except for equipment that had been carefully placed there during the sound check. Brock's guitar sat in a stand by the drums. It looked out of place now that Josie knew the significance of why Brock always carried it on stage with him.

She listened to the announcement about an upcoming event for the fifth time. The announcer had been playing it over again to keep the crowd interested, but even Josie could see they were growing restless as they waited for their star performer.

"I thought you said he'd be out in a minute." Will said, bending toward her ear so she could hear him above the crowd. He was frantic. She couldn't say she blamed him. She should have never left Brock alone.

He'd managed to hide his panic attacks from everyone, including her, until tonight. And he'd truly been alone that day in Galveston. He'd said as much the night they'd made the sandcastle on the beach. It shamed her that in her heart, she hadn't believed him. And it pained her more that he'd lived alone with this secret for so long.

"That's what the man said," she replied, forcing a smile.

Will eyed her. "What did you say to him backstage to make him jumpy? The kid's been fine. This is what we've been working up to and now he's all jumpy."

Josie rolled her eyes. "Brock said he needed a moment. He's not going to skip out on you . . . or his fans."

"He'd better not. There's a lot riding on tonight."

Don't we all know it? She sighed and folded her hands across her chest. Panic attacks could be controlled if a person worked through them. She only hoped Brock had reached the point where he could do that on his own.

The lights started to dim, signaling the show was

about to begin. A lone spotlight bent to the left corner of the stage and within seconds Brock appeared alone. He walked over to the center of the stage and reached for his acoustic guitar.

A grin split Josie's face. He'd changed out of that awful royal blue shirt and into a black T-shirt and black jeans. Perched on his head was the black suede cowboy hat she'd bought for him in Memphis. He walked up to the microphone, wrapped the guitar strap around his neck, and began to fiddle with the strings.

This was the Brock she'd met over a month ago at the studio. This was the man she knew and feared she'd fallen hopelessly in love with. To look at him, no one would know he'd been quaking in his boots back in the dressing room. He was alive with energy, strong and commanding.

"Hello, Nashville!" he yelled into the microphone and the crowd went wild.

"Sorry I kept you waiting. It's good of y'all to come out to see me play. I thought we'd take it a little slow at first, start with a song I wrote in the studio a few weeks back about a woman who's dear to me." Pointing into the darkness as if he could really see her, he said softly, "This one is for you, Josie."

Her heart melted and tears sprang to her eyes as she recognized the song she'd heard that night in the studio when they'd been alone. At the time, she'd known by the way he sang that it was about someone special. She had no idea he'd written it for her.

The small panel light illuminated the soundboard, but Josie had to fight through the moisture in her eyes to see the levels and controls.

Lifting her face to the stage again, she was in awe of Brock. It was clear he had broken free of whatever had gripped him so strongly in the dressing room. Fear had a way of being debilitating. To see him now was amazing. He was so alive with energy. And foolishly, Josie was as star-struck with Brock as all the girls who were screaming his name out in the audience. When the song wound down, Brock stood with a lone white spotlight illuminating him, his head bent to the floor. The crowd was on its feet, going wild.

Brock invited the band on stage with him and they broke into a rowdy, fun number they all loved. It was clear Brock was in his element when he performed. Even if he couldn't see past the first row with the blaring lights blinding him, he was a part of the crowd, lifting his face to the blackness beyond the lights and smiling his appreciation and love for what they were giving him as he played.

He'd written the song for her. The envy she'd felt in the studio was replaced by emotions she didn't want to name. She'd fallen for words before. She knew they could be written and even sung, but still not be heartfelt. How could she believe that this time, the words the man professed to be only for her, were in reality just that?

Chapter Ten

The crowd was still going wild, cheering and chanting Brock's name as he stood backstage and gulped down some bottled water. Still breathing heavily after his last number, Brock poured some cold water from the bottle into his hand and splashed it on his face, wiping away the sweat with a towel someone had handed him.

Miles cracked open a beer, laughing. "Incredible. You were truly magnificent out there tonight. Even I feel like getting up and screaming for you."

Brock chuckled, almost choking on a gulp of water. "Don't you dare try to kiss me or I'll resort to desperate measures."

"Fair enough," he said. "How long are we going to let them scream before we go out for the encore?"

"I say we give it a good long minute," Roy said. "Then they'll go wild when we go back on stage."

Out of the corner of his eye, Brock saw Will standing

at the end of the hall with a man he didn't recognize. Will was animated, his eyes wild with excitement and his hands gesturing rapidly, making his point. Dressed like everyone else backstage, the man could have blended in with anyone who was in the back corridor, but Brock knew Will would only be spending the time to talk with him now if he were something important. Brock guessed the man was Rick Beckley, the A&R executive Will brought in tonight to see the performance. And by the gestures he was making and the smile on his face, Will was happy about the meeting.

It still amazed Brock how quickly the anxiety that had crippled him earlier had vanished once he'd broken free of the chains binding him. He was suddenly looking forward to talking to the man, finding out what he had to say about Brock's performance. But that could wait. There'd be time enough for talk later. First, he wanted to see Josie, to hold her and thank her for being there. No one could have done what she'd done for him.

He dropped the bottled water on the table. "Let's give the crowd what they came here for, boys," Brock said, heading toward the stage door again. There'd be time to talk to executives later. Right now, Brock couldn't wait to get back on stage so he could get personal with the crowd.

A flurry of people swarmed the hallway that led to the dressing room. Josie weaved in and out of the crowd, hoping to see Brock before he was whisked away for private talks with Will and the studio people who'd come to the concert.

Rick Beckley would have to be deaf, dumb, and

blind not to have noticed Brock or the crowd's reaction to him and his music. Brock had been larger than life tonight, moving from one end of the stage to the other, holding the crowd in the palm of his hand the entire performance. It was like nothing Josie had ever seen before. Those that knew Brock fell at his feet, and those that didn't had fallen in love with him tonight and would never forget him.

She'd fallen in love with him long before this though, Josie thought as she made her way through the crowd. The name on everyone's lips right at this moment was Brock Gentry. The laughter and the smiles were all because of him. A good time was had by his new fans.

Flashbulbs popped at the far end of the corridor. Josie couldn't see over all the heads, but her heart picked up a beat. Brock was what they all wanted and she was sure that was where he was now. A smile tipped her lips as she moved, only to freeze when Will caught her hand.

"Josie," he said, pulling her in the opposite direction.

"Great show, huh?" she said, trying to break free.

"Fantastic. Say, we're going to be held up for a few minutes with Rick and his friends at the record company. I was wondering if you could take care of a friend of mine."

Josie stopped dead in her tracks, a frown pulling at her face. "I beg your pardon?" she said sharply.

Will just laughed. "I'm not asking you to date the guy. His name is Ron Albani. He works out of the best studio in Nashville. All the main Nashville players use his studio and the guy has a lot of contacts. I don't want him running away until I have a chance to talk to him a little more. But I can't schmooze both groups at the same time and I don't want to lose the contact, if you know what I mean."

Josie paused. Will reminded her too much of Brian, her boss at DB Sound. There was always some hidden agenda in any request.

His smile wavered. "He mentioned you when he heard Brock's CD and was quite impressed. He's a good person to get to know if you want to move in this industry. I thought you might like the opportunity to meet him."

Josie glanced at the far end of the corridor where Brock was talking with reporters. This was Brock's night. As much as she wanted to share it with him, she didn't want to take him from the spotlight or keep him from making the most of tonight's performance. They'd agreed to meet back at her hotel room later tonight, so there'd be time for them then to celebrate together.

She'd heard of Ron Albani and had to admit she was a little flattered he'd mentioned her name. If, in fact, Will was telling her the truth. Since her purpose for coming on this tour was exactly this, she'd be a fool not to jump at the chance to talk with Ron, if only to get the names of some people in Nashville she could contact on her own. She wanted to meet people who could help her move in a better direction in her career. Ron Albani had the power to do that.

"Why don't you introduce me?" she conceded, pasting on a smile.

There would be time later to share her excitement with Brock. The band would probably party all night and sleep late into the next day. They'd make time, she and Brock.

As she walked with Will in the opposite direction, fear began to brew in the pit of her stomach. Tonight had changed everything for Brock. She only hoped that didn't spell the end for them.

The noise from the street below carried up to Josie's hotel window. She sat in the chair, looking out at the Nashville skyline. Dexter lazily lounged in her lap, where he'd been since she'd returned to her room.

Josie glanced down at her faithful companion and smiled. She was relieved she hadn't been forced to put Dexter in a kennel until she found a permanent home for him. Of course, she didn't have to stay in a hotel at all. She could have chosen to stay on the bus with Dexter rather than put him up with strangers. But tonight, like many other nights she'd stood at the crossroads, she needed her friend.

And she needed Brock. He'd become her friend, not just a man she'd fallen in love with. Josie realized she'd let herself fall into that trap again. But unlike the way things had been with Grant, her relationship with Brock was open and honest and it didn't scare her the way it had with Grant.

Closing her eyes, she sighed, watching the pedestrians below race across the street to avoid the oncoming traffic. A couple walking hand in hand was decked out in evening clothes for a night on the town. She wondered where they were going and if their lives were easy and carefree. She longed for that kind of stability, but inside, she knew her heart followed a path that led her here to Nashville.

Reaching over, she picked up the pictures that had recently been delivered to her room. She sifted through them for the tenth time, smiling as the memories her night on the beach with Brock flooded her mind. Most of the photos hadn't turned out very well because they'd been taken with a flash. But even the blurred and sometimes washed out images made her smile. The time she'd shared with Brock on the beach in Galveston was like a dream from which she didn't want to wake. Tonight had been a lot like that right on the beach.

Tomorrow, they'd both wake up to a new reality. That was the nature of this business. Backstage handshakes had a way of changing your life overnight.

Josie hadn't expected her meeting with Ron Albani to go as smoothly as it had. In truth, she hadn't expected anything at all beyond the introduction. But his enthusiasm for her work—not only with Brock, but with Grant Davies—had her believing the years at DB Sound hadn't undone the strong start she'd made for herself when she'd first come to Nashville all those years ago. That was comforting in a town where you were only as good as your last piece of work and people forgot you as soon as the new act arrived to take your place.

There was promise. She hadn't been offered a job. No, Ron had made that perfectly clear that Pete Harrington liked to be responsible for the hiring of new engineers at the studio. But Ron's word would go a long way toward impressing the owner of the studio. Ron had urged Josie not to wait, to go see Pete as soon as possible and talk to him about coming on board.

The sound of someone leaning on a horn in the traffic below startled Dexter enough to make him leap from her lap and scurry under the bed. With a bittersweet chuckle, she yanked the curtains closed, shutting out the world below. Crawling on her hands and knees over to the bed where Dexter had fled, she pulled up the floral bedspread so she could peer at him. His magnificent eyes glowed back at her and he meowed softly.

"You silly boy, it was just an impatient driver wanting to get home. Nothing but a car horn. Come here and—"

The heavy-handed knock on the door startled her. Dropping the edge of the bedspread, she darted her head up to look at the red glowing letters of the alarm clock. 3:03 A.M. Her smile was immediate. There was only one person Josie could think of who wouldn't wait until morning to tell her something.

Brock. And she was sure he had good news. It had to be.

Rushing to her feet, she glanced in the mirror to give her reflection an approving glance, then raced to the door in her stocking-clad feet. Excitement building, she fumbled with the lock for a few annoying seconds before she was able to throw the door open.

Her smile faded when she saw Miles and Roy standing there.

"You two?"

"Sorry to disappoint you," Miles drawled.

Josie chuckled, and pushed a stray hair away from her face. "Sorry, guys. I just expected—"

"Yeah, yeah, you expected the wonder boy. But if you're waiting on Brock, it's going to be a long night.

Will has him talking to every major player in Nashville tonight."

Her smile spread wider than it had all night, if that was at all possible. "And? What's happening? Tell me everything you've heard!"

Miles and Roy exchanged a look of confusion.

"You mean, you don't know?"

She looked at one, then the other. "No, I don't know anything. I spent most of the night talking to some sound engineer Will insisted I babysit and I missed all the action."

The little fib was lost to Roy and Miles. It hadn't been a hardship to spend time talking with Ron Albani. He'd been gracious and interested in Josie's work. This is what she'd come to Nashville for. Not only had the evening been a huge hit for Brock, but it had been great for her as well. She just hoped that when Brock arrived, they could sort through it all in a way that didn't spell the end of their relationship.

"Nothing's been signed in blood yet, but it's looking that way."

Josie whooped and threw herself into Roy's burly arms, giving him a quick peck on the cheek and then did the same to Miles. "This is fantastic!"

Miles sighed. "Yeah, well . . ."

"Come on, guys! This is great. This is what we've wanted. It's what we've been working for all this time."

Roy nodded, a weak smile tugging against his lips. "Yeah, I know. It looks like a pretty done deal . . . for Brock. The rest of us are still up in the air though."

Confusion collided with her initial joy. "What are you saying?"

"Seems the studio has a different idea of what direction Brock's career should be taking."

A nerve started to twist itself and tightened into a knot in the pit of her stomach.

"And?" she prodded.

Miles couldn't look at her and glanced down the hall. Roy leaned against the doorjamb. "Maybe it wasn't a good idea for us to come here."

"Spit it out. There's obviously a good reason why you felt the need to come to my door in the middle of the night. And don't get cute and tell me it was because you couldn't sleep and needed me to sing you a lullaby."

Miles glanced at her and gave her a quick smile, sympathy in his eyes. "We didn't know how you were going to take the news so we figured we'd come see you before you had a chance to take off without saying good-bye."

She closed her eyes. *Take off? Good-bye?*

She stifled her sigh as best she could, but it escaped despite her best effort. "I would never do that," she said softly, emotion like a tidal wave clogging her throat. Not again, anyway.

Roy reached out and touched her shoulder. "The A&R people from the record company are talking about bringing in their own people to work in the studio. They want to go back and rework all the songs."

She nodded once, folding her arms across her chest. "And?"

Miles and Roy glanced at each other and then to the floor.

"Don't stop now, boys. You're on a roll."

Miles sighed. "They want to finish up the gigs at the Wild Horse Saloon with a new sound engineer, to let him get the feel of Brock's music, before they take Brock on the road again. Will said something about moving in a new direction and tightening his sound instead of making it so . . ."

"Primitive. That was the word he used," Roy added with a roll of his eyes.

Josie fought the urge to shrug the comforting hand Miles had placed on her shoulder. He must have sensed her tension and removed it.

"It's a raw deal and all," Miles added. "Everybody knows that demo you did back in Texas is what got us here."

She laughed at the compliment and shook her head, looking up at the ceiling, then the floor, blinking back the moisture filling her eyes. "Thanks. But it was a group effort all around. I appreciate the support. Will said it was a done deal?"

"No, they're still talking. And for the record, you should know that Brock wasn't buying into it in a big way. But Will . . ."

She sighed and pasted on a smile she didn't feel inside. *Will.* Yeah, he was a carbon copy of Brian all right. He'd thrown her a bone tonight, albeit a fat juicy one, by introducing her to Ron Albani. But it was only so Josie wouldn't make a fuss when he canned her in the morning.

She'd have her meltdown—later. It just wouldn't be now in front of Miles and Roy.

Taking the attention off herself, she asked, "What

about the band? You're still going to stay with Brock, right?"

"The jury is still out on us," Roy added. "These studio execs like to shake things up a bit. But between you, me, and the walls here, I think we're all being replaced."

Chapter Eleven

"**R**eplaced? Everyone?" She'd barely managed to get the words past her throat. Of course, she had known this was a distinct possibility once a record label was interested in taking on Brock. They had their favorite musicians. But, knowing Brock as she did, she couldn't imagine him sitting well with it.

"Yeah, Will was real apologetic and all," Miles said, his voice dripping with sarcasm that didn't show on his face. For all his steam, the man looked like he was about to weep. She was pretty near that herself.

Roy, on the other hand, was just plain ticked. His face grew a hotter glow of red by the moment. "He said he's keeping us for the rest of the sessions at the Wild Horse. Like we have nothing better to do than hang on his tail until he decides what to do with us. I mean, it's not like he can replace us overnight."

"I'm sorry, guys." Stepping aside, she gestured to the room. "Do you want to come in and talk for a bit?"

"You mean, instead of standing out here in the hall like the pathetic losers we are?"

"Stop that," she admonished gently. She'd invited them in to be polite, but deep down Josie hoped they wouldn't take her up on her offer. Rightfully so, they were taking the news hard. But she didn't want to indulge in conversation that was sure to lead to Brock-bashing. Whether he had a say at all in the decision of letting his band go or not—and at this stage of the game, that was still up in the air the ultimate resentment would end up falling on him. Tonight, Brock was the golden kid, the one to envy and hate, no matter how much he was loved by his friends.

She sighed, taking in their drawn faces. On some level, Josie *had* been expecting this. Record companies have their stable of producers and production engineers who gave them what they wanted without any hassle. Josie had yet to elevate herself to that position. *Yet.*

Regardless, the news of being let go so early in the game managed to throw her for a loop and knock her off balance as much as her meeting with Ron Albani had. They still had a few more shows to do at the Wild Horse Saloon. She didn't think that Will would be so quick to replace a band that had become tight in such a short period of time. The band members may not be well known in Nashville, but they were a good fit together. Hopefully, in time, Will and the A&R execs at the record company would see that and decide to keep them together as a band.

"Hey, maybe things will be different for you. You and Brock being so tight and all," Roy added.

Josie shot him a hard look, her jaw tight. It was a knee jerk reaction, born of a long climb to prove herself in a business that cared little about how hard you worked to make it.

"Why should that matter if the record company is set on replacing me?"

Roy shrugged, taken aback by her abrupt words. "I just figured—"

But she cut Roy off. "You figured wrong. My relationship with Brock is as separate from anything we've been doing professionally as yours. If the decision is made to give me walking papers, then I'll be getting them, regardless of my relationship with Brock. I suspect Brock will be by in the morning to give me the news himself."

Miles sputtered. "Don't count on it. He'll probably be sleeping until dinner tomorrow. Will has him on a short string tonight. He's looking to make the most of these contacts."

"As he should. That's what Brock hired him for." She sighed, amazed the tears hadn't appeared. "Look guys, I'm really sorry. You two should be out there with Brock enjoying the evening as much as he is, but sometimes it doesn't work that way. This business is cutthroat. But even if the band is being replaced, you should still be trying to make contacts. Especially if you're going to be replaced. You've still got a week's worth of gigs in Nashville. A lot of people are going to hear about tonight and want to come out to see the shows. And when they do, they're going to see what fine musicians you are and want to work with the two of you. Don't think of it as the end of the world. This is just a jumping point for all of us."

Roy eyed her skeptically, his jaw tight. "You mean to tell me you're not royally ticked off after all the work we've done these past two months?"

She shook her head. "No. I'd be lying if I said I didn't want us to stay together like one big happy family. But I can't change what is happening any more than you can. I can't control it. I can only make the most of the chance being given me. And I intend to do that."

"That's right. I forgot you've been through this before when Grant kicked you to the curb after his contract."

Miles gave Roy a smack against the arm. "Geez, you're such a hard—"

Roy grunted and rubbed his arm. "What'd I say?"

The mention of Grant didn't sting as hard as it might have a few months ago. Or the comment about how she'd been let go. This wasn't the first time she'd been handed a raw deal. But that wasn't the worst of it.

"It's okay, Miles. I can handle it. Yes, I've been through this before and on some level, I was expecting it, even though I'd hoped for better. But I made a mistake once and didn't pursue a good opportunity I was given. I'm not making that same mistake again. Please, don't make that mistake yourselves. Go out there and get a piece of what's coming to you for your efforts. You deserve it."

Josie then said good night, giving each of them a tight hug before closing herself in her room.

The tears didn't come still, but she knew they would. Deep down she expected to be let go. Part of her had fantasized about being beside Brock as he made his rise to fame, sharing the road with him. She pictured the two of them, side by side, traveling the country together.

It had been a nice fantasy. Now it was time to wake up and deal with reality.

Dexter cautiously emerged from under the bed, having recovered from his scare by the window.

"Come here, boy. I need a hug." Reaching down, Josie scooped the cat into her arms and pressed him against her chest.

At least she still had Dex to stand by her. She knew his love was unwavering. He'd always be her faithful companion no matter which road she took.

Brock was dead on his feet. He had shaken so many hands and met so many new faces that his head was spinning.

There'd be time to sort it all out later, Will had said. Well, that may be so. But he didn't think he'd be coming to any new conclusions with the time that was coming.

It was his music, his songs, and yet everyone tonight felt they alone knew what was right for Brock. Brock could see the irony in the situation. In all the years he'd sat in his room and dreamed of living the life of a country musician, he'd been alone. In the beginning, he had been. But he wasn't alone in this anymore. And after tonight, he realized he didn't want to be alone anymore.

The one thing he knew without a doubt he needed in his life was the very thing they were trying to take away—*Josie.*

It wasn't going to happen. No way. He just had to figure out a way to make it right.

The halls of the grand hotel were barren and the bright lights down the corridor only made it seem starker, washing out the décor that had probably cost the hotel a mint in interior design fees. It only magnified the fact that he was a long way from home.

His own house in Steerage Rock was a far cry from clean lined wallpaper and rich colored rugs, plush and patterned with ornate designs. Sure, it had been just as meticulously decorated years before his mother's death, but the main home of the Silverado Cattle Company had her warmth and love etched in every tiny detail and hadn't been changed in over eight years.

Brock had never worn a watch and he didn't plan on starting now that life was going to get out of control. But he knew it was late—no, make that early—enough that he shouldn't be knocking on anyone's door, especially Josie's.

In an hour or two people would be rising from their beds, getting dressed and hustling down to breakfast. They'd be starting their days and Brock was just finishing his. But he needed to see Josie.

She was probably asleep, comfortable and alone in the privacy of her own space for the first time in over a month. He normally would have relished the idea of spending time alone with his own thoughts after being elbow to elbow with the rest of the band. But he needed to see Josie, needed to hold her and just hear her voice. Brock was as sure about that as he was sure he needed his next breath of air.

A quick knock on the door was all it was going to take to satisfy his need. She'd be deep asleep and wouldn't hear his knock, even though he'd wait and knock again. Fatigue would finally win over his desire to see Josie and then he'd retire to his own room alone, and probably sleep until noon. Who wouldn't be able to sleep in a room the size of Texas and in a bed that was a far cry bigger than the bunk he slept in on the bus? Will had promised the luxury as a reward after such a spectacular night.

But sleep wasn't what was on Brock's mind. So much had happened tonight, so much he needed to talk to Josie about. He didn't need a manager or his buddies from the band. What he needed was his friend. And although Josie had become more than just a mere friend to him these past weeks, he knew he needed her to help him sort through everything that was spinning in his head.

As he suspected, his knock had gone unanswered. Leaning his head against the door, he listened to the silence, broken up only by the occasional hum of air passing through the heating ducts. Not even the bell of the elevator interrupted his listening for some sign from the other side of the door.

Brock waited a full minute, then reached his fist to the door again, stopping in mid-motion from knocking. Even though they'd agreed to meet at her room after the show, she was probably asleep. What right did he have to disturb Josie? She wasn't going anywhere tonight and she deserved the reward of uninterrupted sleep in a comfortable bed just like the rest of them.

With a stifled sigh, he pushed away from the door and prayed for the speed of sunrise.

* * *

The tears had come and gone. Josie knew they would. She hadn't stopped them, or even tried to admonish herself for the weakness. This time things were different. She wasn't running.

She'd given herself a good twenty minutes before she could see beyond the blurriness in her eyes to start packing. Why she'd unpacked her clothes from her duffle and put them in the hotel dresser was a mystery to her now. But there was no sense in keeping them there if she didn't plan on spending another night. If she was being fired, then she wasn't in the band's budget anymore and she couldn't afford to stay in a hotel as luxurious as this and pay for it on her own.

Josie tossed her clothes into her duffle bag a little more carelessly than she normally would.

And the tears came again, forcing her to swipe at her face to wipe away the moisture. She dabbed her eyes with a tissue and then blew her nose. Damn the tears. She'd expected the pain and had even accepted it, but she refused to cry in front of Brock or the band. And if she didn't pull herself together quickly, she wouldn't be ready to face any of them in the morning. If she had her way, she wouldn't see another tear at all.

Josie pulled her duffle open wide and started haphazardly stuffing her belongings into it. Since she couldn't sleep, it didn't make sense to wait until morning to pack.

She'd have to look for an inexpensive apartment tomorrow. There'd be newspapers in the lobby. She'd remember to pick one up when they went down for breakfast. Tomorrow at breakfast, she'd see Brock and he'd tell her exactly what was going on. In the excitement of the evening, talk always clouded judgment. Before jumping to the conclusions that were spinning in her head, she'd have to sort things out with Brock.

"What are you doing?"

Startled, she bounced back and landed on her behind on the floor.

Pressing her hand to her chest, she said, "Brock, you scared the daylights out of me."

"The door was open."

Realizing that she had indeed done such a stupid thing in her upset state had her shoulders sagging. "I thought I'd locked it when Miles and Roy left."

He was standing on the far side of the room, staring at her duffle bag on the bed. "You have to be more careful about things like that. You didn't even notice when I walked in. What are you doing?" he repeated.

"Packing."

He laughed one of those are-you-serious kind of disbelieving laughs. "Yeah, I kind of figured that one out. The question is why?"

Well, there's no time like the present, she thought.

"I told you. Miles and Roy stopped by."

Shaking his head, he came into the room fully and shut the door behind him. In the quiet of the night, it sounded unusually loud. "What does that have to do with anything?"

Josie couldn't help the smile that crept up on her face despite the pain she felt in her heart. "I heard all about what happened tonight. How the record company offered you a deal."

"You heard wrong."

She dropped the shirt she'd been holding, tossing it to the bed and advanced toward him.

"Wait. But Miles and Roy said—"

Frustrated, Brock said, "They offered me a recording contract, yes. That much is true."

Hearing it from his own lips made the joy of the news that much more real. "Brock, I'm so thrilled for you."

His eyes wouldn't leave her duffle bag, sitting wide open on the bed, or the clothes that were thrown inside. "That's why you're packing?"

"No, of course not."

"Then why?"

She didn't trust her voice to remain steady. But this man was her friend, if nothing else. "Since I'm being fired, I can't afford to stay at such an expensive hotel on my own. I figured I'd search for something a little more affordable tomorrow after breakfast."

"Miles and Roy told you that you were being replaced?"

"Yes," she said, getting to her feet.

"And you just decided you'd leave. Just like that. Without even talking to me?"

The hurt in his eyes almost leveled her. "No, that's not it at all. I'm not leaving Nashville or you. Just this hotel. And I wasn't going to leave here without talking to you. Brock, are you telling me it isn't true?"

Brock sighed, relief replacing the hurt. "Nothing's been decided. Nothing permanent, anyway. Will was talking so fast I could hardly keep up with him."

"But they want you, right?"

His lips tilted to a grin, but it was bittersweet, as if he was holding back the excitement of that for the prospect of losing his band.

"They want something. I'm just not sure it's me."

She smiled, wanted so much to reach out to him out of joy for his success, yet the troubled look on his face made her reach out for another reason.

"Of course they want you," she said, slipping her arms around his waist. "Who else would they want?"

"I don't know."

Brock waved his hands around in frustration. He should be on top of the world tonight and yet he acted like a man who was about to come unglued, though not in panic, as earlier in the evening. His expression was troubled, like he'd been waging war with himself and lost.

"Will started talking about bringing in some record company techs to do sound at the Wild Horse. Before I knew it, they were talking like it was all a done deal. They wouldn't listen to a word I said after that. I just got a bunch of 'Don't worry, kid. We've got you covered.' replies and a slap on the back."

Josie eased out of his grip, stifling a sigh. "Will didn't listen to you at all?"

"Who do you think was slapping me on the back?"

"Well, then you heard the man yourself, Brock. The news is fabulous for you. They want you. And that's great. They just don't want me."

She picked the duffle up off the bed with one hand and started to zip it shut, but stopped when Brock pulled it from her hands.

"I want you, Josie. I don't happen to agree with Will's

ideas or Rick Beckley's for that matter. When I caught up with Will, I told him I didn't want anything they were offering."

She dropped the duffle on the bed and a few balls of rolled socks fell out along with her toothbrush and makeup bag. She left them there and held onto Brock's hand.

"Are you out of your mind?" she said, taking a step toward him.

"Last time I checked, no."

"You said no? You actually told this record company exec you didn't want a record contract?"

"I said no to the deal he was offering. As far as I'm concerned, we're still negotiating."

Her hands flew to her face. She couldn't believe it. What on earth was he doing? "You said no. Just like that."

Brock pushed his hand over his head, fatigue pulling at his face and clouding his beautiful blue eyes. "I told him I'd think about it and get back to him."

The cockiness in his voice infuriated Josie.

"Brock, you need to get on the phone and call Beckley back. Kiss his feet if you have to, but you don't walk away from a recording contract. That's insanity!"

"What's insane is letting go of my band . . . and you."

"You just don't get it. There are a thousand guys just like you standing outside Rick Beckley's office door just hoping to get a smile from the man. They'd stoop as low as shining his fancy patent leather shoes just to get a moment of his time. And you just said no?"

"Yes." Brock remained calm and that made Josie all the more agitated. Beads of sweat appeared on her forehead and her breathing became as shallow as Brock's had earlier when he'd had his panic attack backstage before the show.

"Brock, he offered you a contract."

"I know."

"You're sabotaging yourself. If you're still in a panic—"

"It has nothing to do with panic." He smiled for the first time since coming into her room. "Thank God you were with me tonight, Josie. I don't think I would have made it on stage at all if you hadn't been here."

"This isn't an offer you can just walk away from that easily. You've got to think about what you're doing. You're good at what you do, but chances like this don't come along as often as the seasons. Most people never get a chance to realize their dreams. You can't make a decision like this without thinking."

"That's what Beckley said, but I have thought about it."

"Yeah, for all of two seconds. Why are you doing this?"

Something jumped in his jaw. "I told you. I don't want to lose you. I love you, Josie."

Her heart melted with his words. She'd wanted so badly to hear them. But for the first time, she realized she didn't need Brock to say it. Even in his tired eyes, his love for her shined brightly.

She shook her head and began to pace around the room. "This isn't about me, Brock. This has never been about me."

"How about us then?"

"I love the idea of us. I really do. I just can't be in the middle of a decision you make about your career. I can't be a reason you would say no."

"Part of what Rick Beckley and his people love, or claim to love, about my music is what you helped me make of it, Josie. What you brought to me. They want to wipe all that clean away and I'm not going for it."

"No regrets. Remember? We said that."

"I remember."

"I can't help but think we made a mistake if you're willing to throw away the chance of a lifetime. And that's what this is, one chance in a lifetime, Brock. You may never get another chance like this."

"I didn't say no. Said I'd think about the offer and gave Rick my terms. Whether you like it or not, you and the band are part of that."

She started to laugh, but tears were surging their way to the surface. She pushed her duffle bag aside and slumped down to the bed. "Don't you realize what's going to happen?"

"It doesn't matter."

"How can you say that? If you start making waves now about the small stuff—"

"I don't consider firing my band small stuff," he said, just as she said, "They're not going to bother with you. They'll find some other smooth, good-looking cowboy to sign the contract they want. Someone who'll do exactly what they want without trouble."

"I don't want what they're offering," he said quietly as he sat down beside her. She reached over and took his hand, ran her thumb over his skin and felt the hot tears slip down her face. "And I'm not signing anything that means you won't be on my team."

Josie's heart swelled with the emotions she'd fought long and hard to hold back. She liked the sound of his words. Josie and Brock, a team. "We're already much more than that, aren't we?" she said, taking his face in her hands and kissing his lips.

"You bet, lady."

As he held her, she fought to find the words to let him see what a mistake he was making. "As much as I want us to be together, Brock, this can't be about me. I won't let it be."

With his forehead pressed to hers, he said, "Like it or not, in a way, it is."

"Well, I don't like it. And I don't like the idea of feeling in limbo as if I'm some groupie hanging around backstage."

"I know. But it'll only be a few days before we can work out the details. I don't think there's much I can do about them replacing you for the next few gigs at the Wild Horse, but I'm going to make sure it's not a permanent thing."

Josie leaned back out of his embrace and looked up at him. "I hope that's true. But in the meantime, I have to be thinking about what I'm going to do if I am replaced for good. We need to think about that."

Brock started to protest, but Josie put a hand gently on his lips to stop his words.

"Look, I met Ron Albani tonight. He was very interested in the possibility of me working at his studio here in Nashville."

"That's great," Brock said. "There's no reason you can't do studio sessions with other musicians."

"Yeah, it's kind of exciting." She bit on her lip. "If they make me an offer to work in the studio, I'm going to take it."

Brock's face hardened. "What do you mean? Like something permanent?"

"Yeah, just in case. There were a lot of industry folks out to see you tonight, Brock. I wouldn't be surprised if the other members of the band hooked up with other gigs as well. What I'm saying is, if it comes down to making the deal without us, you don't have to feel guilty about taking this contract. We're going to be all right. All of us."

The look on his face was one of betrayal.

"Brock, I've always known there was a possibility of this happening. The record companies dictate this sort of thing all the time."

"Nothing permanent has happened yet. Nothing."

"No, but it may be coming to that and I want to be ready for it. I need to keep moving with my career instead of waiting for the other shoe to fall. I've wanted to work in Nashville for as long as I can remember. There's nothing I'd love more than to continue working with you and having you in my life."

Her voice cracked and she took a deep breath to clear it. "I made a huge mistake not following up on my leads the last time I was here with Grant. Instead, I ran away and settled for doing dog food commercials as a way to pay the rent."

Brock simply nodded, his face void of emotion.

"You're right." Sighing, he looked at the floor. "This is a good studio? Good exposure?"

"Yes. Will was the one who introduced me to Ron Albani." The flicker of recognition in Brock's eyes was surely because he'd heard of Ron, not because he was surprised Will had pushed Josie in Ron's direction. Despite her uneasy feelings about Will personally and his feelings about her relationship with Brock, he had been instrumental in setting up the meeting that would jump-start what Josie hoped would be the beginning of a new direction for her in sound recording. She owed Will for that.

Brock ran his hand over his face. "I want to be happy for you and I am. But I don't want to lose you. I just don't want you to give up on me yet."

She turned to him, took his face in her hands and kissed him. "Brock, when I set out on this road trip with you, all I'd hoped to do is get into a Nashville studio and be able to do music again. But as time went on . . ."

She looked at him through her tears. She wanted him to say something. Anything. She couldn't read his mind but right then she desperately wanted to. He couldn't tell her they'd be working together again. Or that they'd be together forever. They were both hanging in limbo, professionally as well as emotionally.

It had taken great strength, but Josie ripped herself from his arms. "This can't be about me, Brock. I won't let it be. If, after everything is said and done and the record company still doesn't want me, you can't say no to them. It'll ultimately destroy us and you know it."

"What are you saying?"

"If another offer doesn't come, then you'll resent me for it. You'll have given up all of your dreams just because some studio exec didn't like your girlfriend. Whatever we started between us will end with bitterness and regret. I won't let you do that. And I won't let our relationship die that way either."

"Our relationship will die? I think we're pretty good together."

"For all your wisdom, you're very naive, Brock."

"Not so much that I don't know what I want."

Brock wrapped his arms around her and she willingly fell into his comfort. His hands tangled in her hair as his mouth brushed over hers in a kiss so powerful, it made Josie's knees so weak she had to cling to him for support. When she thought he was about to let her go, he pulled her even closer instead. "I don't want to let you go," he said.

She pulled herself away from him and walked to the dresser, opening a drawer she'd already emptied and closing it again without really thinking.

"You're not a blue suit man, Brock."

He laughed at her back. "Josie, honey, if you're so bent on that blue suit, maybe I should tell Will to outfit me with one. He's still ticked off I didn't wear that awful shiny thing on stage tonight. He's talking about going shopping again and it always makes me crazy when he does. Anything is better than that flashy getup he has me wear."

"The clothes don't make the man. A blue suit isn't going to change who we both are or how I feel about you."

"I'm not looking to change anything about you, Josie."

"Good, because I feel the same. I wouldn't want you to be anything other than who you are."

"Then what's this about?"

"You said I have a gypsy heart. Well, maybe I do. But somewhere in my heart is the need to have a man come home to me every night. I don't want you to go on the road without me."

"This is what I'm trying to keep from happening."

She buried her face in her hands and blew out a frustrated breath. "I know, Brock. And I love you for it. But what if you can't? Then what? There's going to come a day when you'll go on the road alone and there will be so many pretty girls waiting for you backstage that there will be times you'll forget my name."

"My God, do you even know me? I love you."

Her eyes flooded with unshed tears, and her heart was ripped between joy and heartbreak.

"You wouldn't mean to, but I've seen it happen."

He came toward her and she leaned back against the dresser. "You haven't been listening to those songs at all, have you, Josie? They're all about how I feel for you and how much I want the world to know."

The tears fell freely and she didn't bother to stop them. "I don't want you to write songs for me, Brock. I don't care if the world knows you love me as long as you do."

"And I'm telling you that you're not listening. I'm in love with you. I don't need any of those other women."

"You say that now. But what am I supposed to do? Give up my dreams too? I don't want to have any more regrets. I want to be in your life. But I'm scared that one of us is going to have to give up their dream for the other to succeed. And I don't want to be something in your life that you regret."

"That's never going to happen."

"You say that. I said it once too—a long time ago. I realize the decisions I made were mine and only in part due to Grant. But leaving Nashville the way I did is something I've thought about for a long time. I sold myself out. I don't want you to do the same, Brock. Please, I'm begging you. If it comes down to it, take the deal with Rick Beckley."

"And what? You'll stay in Nashville at some studio while I go on the road alone? We'd never see each other and you just said that was something you didn't want."

"I know," she said quietly.

What she feared more than his leaving without her was watching the span of time between phone calls grow longer and longer until one day, he wouldn't call at all. Her chest ached just thinking about what they'd found together dying a slow and painful death.

"No, Josie. It's not ending here."

"So much is up in the air, my head hurts. You're going to be so busy over the next few days we'll barely have time to see each other. We have to face the reality that may come. Regardless of what happens, I need to set myself up here in Nashville. The sooner the better."

"I'm not saying good-bye to us now, Josie. You're worth fighting for."

She chuckled softly, throwing her hands to her face, not sure if she was going to laugh or cry.

"Don't leave me," he whispered.

Josie shook her head. "I'm not going to leave you.

But this is your fight, not mine. I think it's best if we have a little break until we know for sure what lies in our future. I'm already out as far as the recording company is concerned. I can't do anything to change that."

Brock started to protest, but Josie shushed him with her fingers against his lips. "You've got another week here in Nashville to make the deal. Let's just wait and see what happens."

Chapter Twelve

Brock's room was quiet except for the constant tick of the clock on the wall, counting off the seconds. Every so often, the noise of cars fighting traffic down Main Street outside his hotel window interrupted the steady drone. Pushing the heavy curtains aside, Brock gazed down at the strip's bright neon lights that were screaming with energy and excitement. So much music and magic was present but Brock didn't feel any of that enchantment for himself.

And how could he? Josie was gone. Sure, she was in Nashville tonight, but she wasn't in his arms. When he'd called her hotel room earlier, she hadn't answered the phone.

He closed his eyes to his disappointment. He needed to talk with her and didn't want to wait to meet her at the pub. In public, he couldn't hold her like he wanted to and he needed her to help him sort out all the things that were spinning in his head tonight.

He hadn't seen her much at all over the past few days. Will had filled up his schedule for the week so much he hardly had room to breathe. Tonight he had finally begged off another night of meeting record company people and musicians, telling Will he had other plans with Josie.

Checking his cell phone, he found there were no messages, though he already suspected there wouldn't be one there. He knew she'd be the one to wait for his call. Not because she didn't care or want to see him, but because she did. She wanted to give him space, but he hated every minute without her.

Their first night in Nashville he'd told her he loved her and she didn't say it back. But Brock knew Josie didn't have to say she loved him as much as he loved her. He knew it, felt it in everything she did.

He laughed at the irony, although no one was there to hear it. Josie thought she was doing him a favor by giving him space. He didn't want it though, not from her. The only freedom he ever wanted was to play his music his way—not freedom from the woman who held his life in balance.

But it wasn't fair for him to want her to give up everything she'd dreamed of to travel around with him and watch his success from the sidelines as his dreams materialized and hers faded away. Just as he'd known she'd come on the road with him because she was a gypsy at heart, he also knew Josie wasn't a woman to hang in the shadows and live her life through him. She needed to shine in her own way. It made him all the more determined to convince the record company that he needed Josie by his side in this deal. He wasn't about to give up, not on the deal or on Josie. They'd come too far.

Walking over to the closet, Brock grabbed his denim jacket, pulled it on, and pocketed the key to his room. He'd be early getting to the pub where he and Josie were supposed to meet, but the walls of his hotel room were beginning to close in on him more and he felt more crowded than he had on the cramped bus. He didn't want to be alone.

The boys in the band were out celebrating, as they should be, Brock thought as he walked down the long hall to the elevator. It had taken some doing, but those last few nights of seeing the band play at the Wild Horse Saloon had convinced the record company executives that he had a good team. In the end, they conceded to give the band a chance with the first album and tour, whenever they were ready for that. It was compromise enough for Brock, yet when it came to fighting to keep Josie on as producer and sound engineer, Will lost his steam and negotiations ended there.

As he waited for the elevator to reach his floor, he thought back to the negotiations with the record company.

It had been quite an eye opener for Brock.

The elevator bell sounded and the doors opened up with a whoosh. Guilt ate at him for not seeing what Will had been scheming to do, even though getting Josie out of the picture hadn't accomplished any of the things Will had in mind. All it did was make Brock miss her. He was more determined than ever to prove she was as much a part of the band and his music as he was. But almost as soon as the word *contract* was uttered, Will was talking about Josie's replacement.

The elevator reached the ground level and Brock walked through the lobby of the hotel, barely aware of the people moving around him. Restlessness was running rampant through his veins and he needed space. He didn't quite know how to quell the uneasy feeling, but he knew it wouldn't disappear if he was stuffed in a hotel room all alone.

As he pushed out onto the sidewalk and saw the lights down on the strip, he decided the only way to rid himself of this feeling was to get out and be with people. He walked across town to Josie's hotel, figuring he could catch her before she left, but his disappointment only grew when she didn't answer her door.

He walked a few blocks toward the noisy corner pub. The bright neon lights posted above the door read THE LAZY DOG LOUNGE. Josie had told him on the phone that she'd eaten lunch here a few times and the food was good. Maybe he could convince her to get the food to go so they could bring it back to the hotel and spend some time alone.

A young couple barreled through the double doors onto the sidewalk, laughing hard and then embracing with a kiss. A twinge of envy stabbed at him, making him sigh and look away. He wanted this closeness with Josie.

He pushed through the door into the crowded pub, weaving through people milling about, looking to see if Josie had also come early. But she was nowhere to be found and on the second pass through the pub, his eyes were drawn to the empty stage. A drum kit sat in the shadows behind a lone microphone. An acoustic guitar was snug in a stand on the right side.

Brock had wanted to play his music for so long. In all the dreams he'd had growing up, he'd been alone. There'd never been anyone sharing the spotlight with him. No one stood beside him on stage. Now he couldn't imagine facing the road without Josie. When had she gotten so important to him that those dreams didn't seem right without her? But they didn't. He'd fallen in love with this incredible woman he wanted by his side so badly he couldn't wait for her to come walking through those doors.

"Table for one, sir?" the hostess asked. Brock barely noticed the young girl, keeping his eyes focused on the stage as if it were calling to him.

He shook his head. "I'm meeting someone. I'll just sit at the bar until she gets here. Is there a band playing tonight?"

The hostess gave a brief glance over her shoulder toward the stage. "Only on the weekends."

"Do you think the manager would mind if I played a short set while I wait?"

With raised brows, she eyed him up and down. Brock wanted to laugh. She probably thought he was a vagrant looking to play for a meal. He liked the idea of no one knowing him, coming into a bar and just playing for fun.

He couldn't imagine a day when he wouldn't be able to walk these streets without being recognized, without someone snapping his picture or asking for his autograph. But if success followed on the heels of their success at the Wild Horse Saloon, it would happen.

Right now, Brock was just happy that the world didn't know his name or face yet.

"Uh, you'll have to talk to the manager about something like that. He's usually pretty fussy about who performs here."

She motioned for him to an empty stool at the bar before disappearing for a moment. Inside of a minute, she resurfaced at the end of the bar with a man and pointed to Brock. Through the haze, he saw the manager look him over pointedly. The white noise of idle chatter and laughter made it impossible to hear what he was saying, although from the look on his face, Brock guessed he'd drawn the same conclusion as the hostess.

The manager stalked over to where he was sitting. "You asked to see me?"

"Mind if I borrow a guitar? I'm waiting on a friend and thought I'd play for a while." He motioned with his thumb out the door. "My band and I are staying at a hotel just up the street."

The manager shifted his jaw to one side and scrutinized Brock in a sidelong glance. "How do I know you're any good? You might drive away my customers."

"I just finished a gig at the Wild Horse Saloon and feel like playing for a small crowd tonight, is all. I tell you what. Let me play one song and if the crowd doesn't mind I'll keep going. Sound fair?"

The man shrugged. "Wild Horse Saloon, huh? Knock yourself out. Have you eaten?"

"Not yet. Like I said, I'm expecting a friend to come by in a bit."

"When you're done, take a look at the menu." He waved a waitress over. "It's on the house," he called to the waitress over the noise. She nodded and then went back to her paying customers.

Brock knew he could have easily played his guitar alone in his hotel room until it was time to meet Josie. But back at the hotel, he wouldn't hear the hum of the room or feel the intimacy of sharing his music. That's all he'd wanted his whole life. He didn't need to be a star. He just wanted to play.

Within minutes of getting the manager's approval, Brock was climbing onto the stage. He was worlds away from the panic he'd felt the other night at the Wild Horse. The crowd wasn't interested in him or what he was doing. They were talking, laughing, and enjoying their dinners. He was just in the background, part of the wallpaper. They didn't know his name and quite frankly, Brock didn't care. If they enjoyed the music while they ate their dinners and had a few drinks, that was fine by him.

Brock selfishly played for himself tonight.

With the first strum of the guitar, he tuned out the chatter of the crowd and sang the song he'd written for Josie, knowing she couldn't hear him. Still, he kept his eyes fixed on the door, waiting for her to appear.

Josie's stomach growled as she stood outside the small pub at the end of Main Street. She was hungry and tired from searching all day for apartments and couldn't wait to tell Brock about the new place she'd found.

She needed his comfort too. Getting Dexter settled

in a local shelter had been harder on her than on the cat. As her faithful companion had been placed in the kennel, Josie felt like her arms were being ripped from her body. But now that she'd found a nice apartment, Dex would be coming home to whatever home she created soon.

A small group of people bustled through the door to the street. She waited for them to exit the pub before making her way inside. Before she even had a chance to enter, however, she heard Brock's voice over the microphone.

Brock was gone for good.

A tear trickled down her cheek as she watched from the front of the pub to the stage beyond the dinner crowd. He stood on the stage, playing his songs like she'd never heard them played before. The raw emotion with which he sang each word was lost to the people sitting at the tables having their dinner. He was alone and Josie was sure he hadn't seen her yet. She longed to rush right up to the stage to tell him the words she couldn't say before. She loved him.

But the sadness in his voice, the torment in his eyes told her a story the words of his song didn't. He hadn't been successful getting the record company to agree to keep her on and it was eating at him.

She wasn't running. Not this time. Her appetite suddenly gone, she waved to Brock to get his attention as the song wound down. His smile was bittersweet.

"When are you leaving?" she asked as they met in the middle of the pub.

Brock reached up and touched her face. "Tomorrow."

* * *

The console was bigger and newer than the one she'd been used to at DB Sound. There was no duct tape covering the splits in the padding or any makeshift speakers. This studio was state of the art for serious business. The fine wood panels gave the room a light and airy feeling. Josie thought of all the music stars who'd stood on the other side of the glass wall and sang the hit songs she'd heard on the radio since she'd been a child.

She'd gotten what she'd wanted. She'd made it to Nashville. No matter how angry her mother had been with her for leaving, Josie knew she'd be proud to know she'd made her dreams come true. She only had one regret left and that was that her mother would never know Josie's success.

Regardless of whether her mother could remember her or not, Josie decided it was time to remember her roots. She'd be moving into her new apartment over the weekend. Dex could come out of the kennel and would protest only slightly until he became acclimated to his new home. But after that, she'd arrange for monthly trips to Texas to visit her mother.

She'd thought of moving her mother to a facility in Nashville, but after years of being at her present nursing home, she'd made friends with the nurses and other patients. It wouldn't be fair to selfishly want to have her in Nashville just to make it convenient for Josie to visit.

But even though her mother didn't remember Josie as her daughter, it was important for her to establish a new relationship. Josie was determined to be there for her mother in any capacity she could.

"Can I help you?"

Josie turned to find a man coming into the studio. He

was old enough to be her grandfather, with a kind face and a big smile. How different it would be to work in a place like this.

She extended her hand. "Josie Tibbs. I spoke with Ron Albani last week backstage at the Wild Horse Saloon." Awareness dawned on his face and Josie felt her spirits rise for the first time since she'd said good-bye to Brock.

"You were touring with that new fella Ron went on about. I've been waiting for you to stop by. Ron said you were looking for a job in a studio."

He shook her hand and introduced himself as Pete Harrington, the owner of the studio. His smile remained.

Now that it was certain she wouldn't be going back on the road with Brock, she needed something permanent.

"Yes. I've just relocated to Nashville and am looking for steady studio work."

"What experience do you have?"

Josie was prepared for this question. She'd rehearsed it a thousand times in her head. There was a time she would have bitten off her tongue rather than mention her association with Grant Davies. But it was part of her resume. His name opened doors. What she did when she walked through that door was up to her.

"I've done some studio work lately with Brock Gentry and I worked with Grant Davies on his early work. I've brought some CD's, both live performances and studio work."

"We'll have a listen to those in a minute. But I must tell you, I trust Ron's judgment. It's not often he talks my ear off about a new talent. You really impressed him."

She couldn't keep the smile from her face.

Pete sighed. "Unfortunately, I don't have the need for another full-time sound engineer. I can give you a job, but it'll be ground floor, basically whatever sessions aren't spoken for by my longtime engineers, possibly as an assistant if they like what you can do. It'll be mostly grunt work. Does that sound like something you can handle?"

She nodded. "I'm willing to start at the bottom, if that's what it takes." She'd do boring dog food commercials again if she had to. She was willing to pay her dues if it meant she'd be able to eventually work in music again.

He chuckled. "I have a feeling you won't stay there very long. We have a lot of influential music industry folks pass through these doors. You might pick up some time working with them on the side. If you're as good as Ron said, word will get around and you'll be taking your pick of sessions."

Josie left the studio with a smile and a dull ache in her heart. This is what she'd wanted. She'd come back to Nashville and landed a job in a good studio that would give her a chance to advance in her career.

But as the door closed behind her and she felt the cool air hit her face and the smell of fried food assault her nose, she couldn't help but think of Brock.

She could go about her day. Lord knew there was a long list of things she had to get done before she started working. She needed to have her things trucked over from Texas. She needed to pick up the keys to her new apartment and then get Dexter out of the kennel. She'd sleep on the floor for a few days until her furniture arrived. There was so much to keep her occupied. But she had a feeling that no matter how she filled her day, her mind and her heart would be seeking out Brock.

She was in Nashville because of him and because of the confidence he'd had in her ability. His friendship had helped her break out of the chains holding her back. She wanted to call him and share the news with him, but it would have to wait until late tonight. He'd call if he was free. He'd left this morning and was probably doing a sound check in whatever city Will had scheduled him in tonight. She'd check her messages when she got back to the hotel just in case there was a change of plans.

Josie crossed the street and started walking the eight blocks to the hotel, all the while fighting with herself about whether or not she should call. His cell number was burning a hole in her pocket. In the end, she decided against it. They'd said their good-byes this morning as if it wasn't the last time, but Josie knew it was only a matter of time. They both had to move on. Both of them had new beginnings. Alone.

"Are you out of your mind?" Will boomed as they left the conference room. Pointing to the room where their private talk had taken place, he continued in a quieter tone. "This is what we've been working for. You don't just walk into a major record label office and start making demands until after we've agreed on a deal. They're ready to hand you everything you want on a silver platter."

"No, Will. I never agreed to this, which is why I insisted on another meeting before we signed. What they're offering is everything *you* want. Not me. I have to admit I'm to blame in part for some of this. We haven't been communicating too well, you and I."

"What are you talking about?"

"It's taken me far too long to figure it out, but you and I don't see me the same way."

"For instance?"

"You were the one to broach the subject of changing the band around."

"I thought we settled that. You wanted the band back and they agreed."

"All except for Josie."

Will's eyes narrowed. "Josie put you up to this," he accused.

"Actually, I can come to conclusions pretty well on my own." Brock tried to keep his irritation from getting the better of him. He hadn't been quick to see the rift between Will and Josie and for that he was sorry.

"What does that woman want? I set her up with a sweet deal. Her own career is going to explode!"

Brock laughed. "You think that was all your doing? Don't pretend that she didn't have anything to do with where she is right now. She's good at what she does, which is why I wanted to work with her in the first place."

"And that's all?"

"That's all you need to know. The rest of it is none of your business."

Will shook his head and laughed hard. "Everything about making you a star is my business, kid. You haven't been around this town long enough to know how it works. You don't see things like I do."

"You're right. Because you're taking me somewhere

I don't want to go. This is bad timing, I know, but there need to be some changes with us."

Brock stood a few inches taller than Will, but as Brock straightened his back, it wasn't the extra height that gave him the advantage. It was his resolve to make some changes.

"For starters, I'm not 'the kid.' You can make my image into anything you want as long as you see me as a partner and the image is something we both agree on. That's number one if we're going to be working together."

Will seemed momentarily affronted by the notion, staring at Brock with wide-eyed disbelief.

"I'm not wearing flashy clothes, or allowing you or anyone else to mold me into what they want as if I'm some Gumby doll. You can get anyone to be that for you, Will. But that's not what I am and not the way I want people to see me. I don't want to be hiding behind all that glitz."

"This is Nashville, Brock. This town loves all that glamour."

"Then I guess they don't want me."

Will actually swayed. "You're talking about throwing away a record contract? Listen to what you're saying."

"I'm hearing myself just fine, Will. And if all this record company wants is a fake face and a puppet, they can find it in someone else. You know what I want. If they want me, they're taking me on my terms. Otherwise 'the kid' is walking."

The day had started out sunny with a promise to stay that way. Not that Josie had enjoyed any of it, however.

Dexter would be flaming mad at her when she got home.

She'd wrapped up her first solo session, another radio spot. It had gone off without a hitch and her client seemed happy. It didn't sting as much as she'd thought it would, and Pete seemed impressed that she'd done well. Josie only hoped her work had impressed him enough to want to move her into some real studio work soon. *Everything in its time*, she thought.

Josie had foolishly thought that a change of scene wouldn't bring on memories of Brock. There were new people to meet, fresh faces, and different procedures. She had plenty to keep her mind occupied on anything other than missing Brock.

She'd been wrong. They'd spent time in the studio and had shared moments on the road. Though miles away from where it all started, this studio still brought back memories of those late night sessions with Brock.

Lost in her own thoughts as she straightened out the equipment in the sound room, Josie didn't hear the door open and then shut.

Her thoughts were broken by the sound of footsteps in the hallway.

"Is that you, Pete?" she called, walking out front. She was eager to talk to him about her next session. But it wasn't Pete.

"I can't believe I almost forgot how beautiful you are," Brock said, his smile slightly askew and that dimple she'd seen the first day teasing her.

Her breath caught in her throat and she felt the pounding of her heart against her ribs. "You can do better than that, cowboy," she said. "You look good."

He ran a hand down the front of his dark tweed jacket and unfastened the button to reveal a black buttondown shirt tucked into black jeans. The black cowboy boots he wore were brand new.

"Yeah? Will and I made a compromise. I'll dress up nice as long as I don't look like a clown."

"This suits you much better."

"I think so."

Laughing, she launched herself into his arms. It felt good to have him holding her again. She'd missed his face and the deep timbre of his voice that had comforted her on their journey from Texas to Nashville on more nights than she could count.

"Please say you're staying in town for a few days," she said, almost afraid the answer would be no. After all the publicity generated by the show in Nashville, Josie was sure Will had lined up a string of gigs at much larger venues than they'd had in the past month. For days after the Wild Horse Saloon gig, Brock had been the talk of Nashville musicians.

His arms were still wrapped around her as he bent his head lower to give her a kiss. "I'll be in town for a little while. I'm going back into the studio to do some additional tracks. I've got some new songs that I think are a better fit for an album."

Her heart pierced. She wouldn't be there this time to share that experience with Brock.

Rallying some enthusiasm she didn't feel, she said, "Oh. That's great."

Smiling, Brock glanced around the studio. He pulled away from her and walked into the sound room before turning back again.

In her wildest dreams, Josie never imagined it would be so hard to be this close to Brock and not touch him. Just those few moments in his arms had her longing for more. Memories of his gentle hand on her back flooded her mind. The way his lips touched hers with a heated passion so strong she thought she'd burn to ash.

She wanted to follow Brock, hang on his heels. No, she wanted him to hold her again. Instead, she tied her hands in a knot around herself.

"How do you like this place?"

"The studio is state of the art, like no place I've ever worked."

"Good, then I'll have to make sure we book some time here if they have the space available."

"You'll have to talk to Pete about that. He does all the scheduling."

Maybe he'd put her on as a second to assist whomever the record company brought in to work with Brock. It wouldn't be the same as how it had been in Texas. She wouldn't be the one to produce or run the show, but it would give her a chance to be with Brock again and have him close by for a while.

His dark eyes swept over her, penetrating her to the very core as if he could read her mind.

"How long are we going to dance around this, Josie? I'm dying here."

He opened his arms wide and as she laughed, she flew into his embrace again. He felt so good and suddenly all the uncertainty of leaving him seemed to melt away.

"I'm dying here too, Brock. But if working in this studio is a way to keep you in town for a while, then I'm all for it. I've missed you."

"Me too. But we won't have to be apart anymore."

Startled by his words, her eyes flew open wide. "What?"

"I couldn't do it, Josie. I couldn't sign that contract if it meant losing you."

She stared up into his face and sighed. "You didn't take the contract? Brock, I don't want to be the reason you have regrets."

"Yeah, you said that. But no matter what you thought I was leaving behind, lady," he said, tipping her chin up with his fingers, "I would have regretted losing you more." And then his mouth came over hers and he crushed her against his chest in a warm embrace she never wanted to end. Breathing him in, she realized she'd missed him more than she'd allowed herself to acknowledge these last few days. But now he was here, he was real, and she couldn't imagine the thought that he'd go away again.

Still, this wasn't just about her. It was about what Brock had given up to be with her. A tear slid down her cheek. "This is something that's going to follow you. I can't believe you turned down that record deal."

He lips tilted into a grin. "Oh, I didn't turn down the deal completely, I just kept holding out until they agreed to my terms."

Her mouth flew open in shock. "Really?"

He laughed. "You should have seen Will's face when I told the boys to go back to the drawing board and write up a new contract because I wasn't giving up my gypsy."

Josie's hands flew to her face. "Oh, please tell me you didn't say it like that, did you?"

Laughing, Brock said, "No. I just told it like it was.

You and I have something special here, Josie. Not just in the studio, but like this, when I'm holding you in my arms. No matter what deal they put on the table, I would have regretted not fighting for what was right. And that means keeping you by my side in every way. We'll never have to be apart again."

Her heart swelled. "You mean that?"

He nodded, his blue eyes gazing into hers.

"Will probably hates me."

"He'll get over it. I'm sorry I didn't see him pushing you around like he was."

She shrugged. "I can hold my own, Brock, if you haven't noticed. And Will was just looking out for his interests."

"And I'm looking out for mine. So what do you say? Do you really want to chain yourself to Nashville?"

She wrapped her arms around his shoulders. "I'd rather chain myself to you, Brock Gentry."

He raised both eyebrows with interest. "I like that idea. Say you'll marry me, Josie."

Shocked at his sudden proposal, she pulled away and stared at him, but he just held on tighter to keep her from fleeing.

"If you're still stuck on marrying a blue suit man, I'll buy that blue suit and wear it just for you. As long as you're with me, I don't care what I'm wearing."

She kissed his lips with a promise in her heart that what she'd been looking for all her life was what she had in her arms at that very moment. "Forget the blue suit. I love you just the way you are."

He cocked his head to one side. "What was that?"

"What?"

"That thing you just said."

She smiled, her whole heart and soul bursting. "I love you, Brock Gentry."

He nuzzled her neck with a kiss. "I was wondering when you were going to get around to saying those words to me."

"I love you. I'll say it as many times as you want me to for the rest of our lives."

"Thank you, God," he said. "And just for the record, I'm a man who likes coming home to the same woman each and every night. I don't care where we make home, I just know that's where I'll be if I've got you in my arms. There will always be women at every gig, pulling at me. Is that something you can handle?"

"Don't put your feelings in a song, Brock. Just tell me what's in your heart. Just like this. I want to know it and feel it from you. Do you love me?"

"You'd better believe it, lady. More than life itself."

Blue suit be damned. "Then that's enough for me."